Alec Baldwin
Doesn't
Love Me

Alec Baldwin Doesn't Love Me

Other Trials of My Queer Life

MICHAEL THOMAS FORD

alyson books
NEW YORK

Manufactured in the United States of America.
Printed on acid-free paper.

This trade paperback original is published by Alyson Publications Inc.,
P.O. Box 4371, Los Angeles, California 90078-4371.
Distribution in the United Kingdom by Turnaround Publisher Services Ltd.,
Unit 3 Olympia Trading Estate, Coburg Road, Wood Green,
London N22 6TZ, England.

First edition: January 1998

05 06 07 08 09 a 12 11 10 9

ISBN 1-55583-431-0
ISBN-13 978-1-55583-431-9

Library of Congress Cataloging-in-Publication Data
Ford, Michael Thomas.
    Alec Baldwin doesn't love me & other trials of my queer life / Michael
        Thomas Ford.
    1. Homosexuality—Humor. 2. Gay men—Humor. 3. Gay wit and
        humor. I. Title II. Title: Other trials of my queer life.
    PN6231.H57F67 1998
    814'.54—dc21   97-46050 CIP

Contents

Author's Note . . . . *vii*

My Queer Life

Diary of a Would-be Porn Star *3*

Too Much of a Good Thing *12*

Adult Education *17*

Dyke the Halls *26*

Taking the Credit *35*

The Nonwriting Life *44*

Men and Other Obstacles to Happiness

How Alec Baldwin Ruined My Life *53*

The Sound of Music *61*

Why I Hate Shopping *70*

The Perils of Dating *77*

Picture Imperfect *84*

When I Grow Up *90*

Adventures Among the Straight People

Trial by Fire *101*

Singing a Different Tune *114*

Homo Improvement *119*

A Model Queer *125*

Separation Anxiety *133*

Cyberslut *141*

The Way I See It

No Splashing in the Gene Pool! *151*

Games People Play *159*

A Sporting Chance *167*

Just One of the Girls *176*

I'm Not Saying It's Wrong... . . . . *184*

A Slightly Dented Childhood

If Jesus Loves Me, Why Hasn't He Called? *195*

Confessions of a Don't-Bee *205*

Packing for the Second Coming *214*

The Crown of Heaven *223*

The Theory of Relativity *233*

Saying Good-bye to Grandma *242*

Author's Note

TRUTH IS ALMOST ALWAYS STRANGER THAN FICTION, AND I have often been told that I have a very strange life, although to me it has generally seemed perfectly ordinary. This, of course, is the paradox of having odd experiences — you don't realize how truly odd they are until you tell someone else about them and then see that look of disbelief staring back at you. Only then do you begin to think that maybe something queer is going on after all.

The pieces in this book are all true. Well, mostly. At the heart of each one is a piece of reality. My reality, anyway. I've heard people say that being queer doesn't affect how you view the world. I beg to differ. I don't think you can grow up in this place as a gay person without developing an interesting perspective on things.

Here, then, are some pictures of life as I see it, ranging from the childhood days when I was convinced Jesus was going to come and snatch me up into the clouds to more recent adventures navigating the waters of being a queer person in America today. As anyone who's ever looked around can tell you, it's a weird place.

Many thanks must go to Kathleen Vickery, late of *Our Own* newspaper, and to Margaret Maree, who first suggested I write the My Queer Life column and then encouraged me to syndicate it. The same goes for Robert

Thomson and Jim Armstrong of *Fab* magazine, who let me rant every issue in my The Way I See It column. Thanks also to the other editors at magazines, Web sites, and newspapers across the country who gave me a place to tell my stories. (By the way, I'm still waiting for the checks.)

None of this would have happened without Katherine Gleason, who all along has said I have the most peculiar life of anyone she knows and insisted I put it all down; and Gerry Kroll, who kindly believed me when I said people would be interested in reading about it. And I am, I suppose, especially indebted to my family and friends, who are responsible for many of the events in this book. I told you I'd get even some day.

My Queer Life

Diary of a
Would-be Porn Star

For a short time a few years ago, I reviewed porn movies for a now-defunct magazine. Once a month a package would arrive, discreetly wrapped in brown paper, containing five or six new flesh flicks for me to watch and give my opinions of. The pay was almost nonexistent, but I did it anyway, happy to be able to do my part in educating the smut-viewing public about the merits of these fine pieces of cinematic beauty. "Anything for art," I told my friends when they pretended to be appalled.

Watching these entertaining videos provided more than the occasional moment of pleasure, but after a while I had a disturbing thought: None of the things I saw in the movies ever happened to me. Oh, sure, the men in the films did things that I did. They went to the beach. They went grocery shopping. They took their dogs for walks. But that's where the similarities ended. When I took my dog for a walk, no handsome man asked me if I needed help burying my bone. When I returned books to the library, the shy man behind the desk didn't follow me into the periodicals section and show me his Dewey decimal system. It just didn't happen.

Because I firmly believe that life imitates art, I knew that the filmmakers couldn't possibly be lying. Surely all across America, men were having hours of hot, oily fun with pool boys, pizza deliverymen, and neighbors they happened to meet in the hall while wearing nothing but a jockstrap. Behind every bush there had to be two guys engaged in carnal knowledge of each other with barely a hint of polite introduction preceding it. Clearly, I was just going about things the wrong way.

I decided that with a little effort, my life too could be as exciting as a porn movie. Even better, it could actually be a porn movie. All it would take was a little bit of planning and some derring-do. If I just put my mind to it, I would soon be romping from one exciting sexual encounter to another. I anticipated days of endless orgies with beautiful men who fulfilled my every fantasy.

I chose a Friday to begin my new life, since I had deduced from my film watching that on Fridays everyone in North America becomes incredibly horny and ready for fun. I woke up that morning raring to go and leapt from my bed in search of the first orgasm of my porn-star life. Wearing nothing but my bathrobe, which was strategically left hanging open so that any men I happened to encounter would have easy access, I strolled to the front door and opened it.

Now, I'm sure the paperboy (who of course had just celebrated his eighteenth birthday) didn't mean to scream as loudly as he did. Still, at such an early hour, it was a little unsettling. And certainly there was no need for running away in such a hysterical manner and leaving all of those papers on my lawn. As I shut the door, I made a mental note not to leave a tip at Christmas. In porn films the paperboy was always most accommodating. To find that mine wasn't was a bitter disappointment indeed.

I decided I was going to have to take a much more active approach if I was going to be successful at porn stardom. I sat down and made a list of the most popular locations for finding sex, based on the porn films I'd seen. The list went like this (in order of frequency):

1. Apartment complexes in Laguna Beach.
2. Beaches on deserted islands.
3. Gyms.
4. Locker rooms in high schools after football practice.
5. Video stores (X-rated sections).

This, as you might well imagine, was not entirely helpful. California was on the other coast. Deserted islands are hard to come by. And high school administrators are not frequently as open-minded as one might think. In the end the gym and video store were the only real possibilities. I decided to try the gym first, since the video store didn't open until noon and I was ready for action immediately. Throwing on some shorts, I packed up my bag and left.

The gym at 9 o'clock in the morning bore little resemblance to the stud-filled athletic facilities of my porn-viewing experiences. Instead of rooms crammed with well-built men wearing tight shorts, no supportive gear, and lots of oil, I found myself surrounded by fifty-two middle-aged women in floral-print leotards and headbands gyrating to Paula Abdul while attempting to get in shape for their daughters' weddings. It was hardly the stuff of homo fantasy.

Undaunted, I checked out the sauna, which, according to porn movies, was frequently the site of some vigorous groping. Inside, it was just as misty and hot as the porn films had promised. And hidden within its steamy interior, a scantily clad man was reclining on one of the wooden benches. Casually carrying my towel (no one wears them in porn movies), I went in and sat down next to him. To my satisfaction he was quite a looker. Just my type.

I nodded, and he smiled. In porn movies this always means, "I want to suck your cock." So I did what any good porn star would do — I spread my legs and waited for him to pounce.

"Hey," he said, putting a hand on my waiting thigh, "have you ever read the *Book of Mormon*?"

I was out of there in a flash, leaving my towel behind as I hightailed it onto the street. This was not the way things were supposed to go. I checked my watch — only fifteen minutes until the video store opened. I started walking.

Entering the store, I ducked behind the black curtain separating the adult videos from the rest of the store. To my surprise and joy, a cute college jock type was busily looking at the covers of the boxes. I looked at the one in his hand and, seeing that it featured two men and not a silicone-laden, red-lipped woman, congratulated myself on my good luck.

I played it cool, knowing full well that these things had to involve a little bit of play before the kill. I walked a few feet down the row and picked up a tape. Out of the corner of my eye, I could see that Mr. Frat Boy was taking quick glances my way. I moved closer, reaching for a tape near him.

"That one isn't so good," he said.

He'd taken the bait. "Really?" I said. "Is there one you like better."

He turned and smiled. "Why? You interested?"

6

Finally. Sex was imminent. "Maybe," I said, already ripping his rugby shirt off and sucking on his nipples in my mind.

He looked around to make sure we were alone. "I really like to do it to *The Little Mermaid,*" he said. "Disney makes me hard as a rock. Especially if you can talk like the crab."

Clearly, it wasn't my day. I suddenly remembered somewhere I had to be and excused myself before Jocko could launch into a chorus of "Under the Sea."

As I walked home, I pondered my plight. I couldn't understand why it was so hard to get laid. In porn movies men with brontosaurus-size erections practically fell out of the sky. It was impossible to turn a corner without tripping over a luscious piece of beefcake, rump in the air and ready for fun. But all I seemed able to find were the rejects who never made it past Dropping and Sucking 101.

Back in my own home, I tried to think what Ryan Idol would do in my situation. After a minute it came to me. I picked up the phone and dialed the cable company.

"Something seems to be wrong with my box," I said when the weary operator's voice crackled through. "It isn't working. Can you send a guy over?"

Much to my delight, it worked. The operator said a man would be by in about twenty minutes. I hung up, thanking the porn gods, who obviously had decided to smile upon me after all. I then raced into my bedroom and set the trap. I grabbed a tape from the pile by the VCR, shoved it in, and hit PLAY. My plan was simple: I would pretend the cable was out. When the technician tried to turn on the television, a porn film would be playing. Then I'd make my move. I'd seen it once in a movie, and it worked brilliantly.

I paced around the apartment until I heard a knock on the door. Still wearing my gym shorts, I opened it. Standing outside was a hunky young stud fair near bursting out of his uniform. I ushered him inside. His shirt had BILL stitched on it.

"Right this way," I said in what I hoped was a husky voice dripping with innuendo. "I'm not sure what's wrong."

I led Bill into the bedroom, where he went straight for my cable box. I watched as he turned it on and off, checked the wiring, and did something with a little tool he pulled out of his back pocket. He never once turned the TV on.

"That should do it," he said, turning to go.

"Wait a minute," I yelped. "Shouldn't you check it? I mean, what if it's not fixed?"

"Oh, it's fixed," he said. "Trust me." He headed for the door.

"No!" I yelled, practically pushing him back into the bedroom. "Please, just check it."

Bill gave me an odd look as he turned on the television. I held my breath, waiting for a shot of Zak Spears doing what he does best to appear and get the ball rolling, as it were. Instead what came on was a close-up of Mary Tyler Moore tap-dancing madly in an elevator in *Thoroughly Modern Millie.* Her big toothy grin spread across my TV where Zak's hard-as-iron cock should have been thrusting in and out of some lucky orifice.

"Happy?" Bill asked, glaring at me.

Dejected, I nodded. It just was not meant to be. I watched as Bill left the house, pulling the door shut behind him.

8

"You bitch!" I screamed at Mary as I turned the tape off. "Why couldn't you at least have been a come shot?"

I was running out of possibilities. It was now midafternoon, and I still hadn't gotten off. I sat down to think, wishing bitterly that I had an outdoor pool to lounge beside naked, a gardener with poor English skills and hours of staying power, or at least a handsome neighbor whose wife just didn't like to do certain things. But all I had was a faulty sprinkler, a pimply kid who raked up the leaves once every October, and old Mrs. Krumbach, who complained ceaselessly about her joints. The stuff of wet dreams, my life was not.

Then I had an idea. I'd once seen a movie in which a young man had engaged in a stimulating encounter with another man in the men's room at the local mall. Surely I could do that too. I hustled out the door to the local galleria. Then it was but a quick turn past the Sunglass Hut to the rest room. I threw open the door and commenced scouting out my lucky partner.

There were a couple of possible candidates lined up at the urinals along one wall. I picked the one who seemed the most pornlike (he had on work boots, which I was convinced was a sign) and squeezed in next to him. As I unzipped I tried to remember what the actor in the movie had done. I casually looked over at my neighbor and smiled slightly.

"Hey," I said.

"Hey," he said, smiling back.

I had no idea what to do next. I couldn't for the life of me remember how it had been done in the movie. I reached inside my fly so I could at least pee and pretend to be doing something. But there was no fly. As I scratched around frantically inside my jeans, I realized that in my haste to leave the gym earlier in the day, I'd put my boxers on backward.

Mortified, I tried to free myself from my underwear. My waiting partner watched as I ran my hand around inside my pants, looking for a way out. I looked at him and tried to manage a lighthearted chuckle. Hoping to distract him, I winked seductively.

My contact tumbled out of my eye and fluttered gently into the urinal, where it swirled around in the water, bobbing over the fluorescent pink disinfectant tablet like an inner tube. I squinted, trying to locate it while simultaneously attempting to rearrange my boxers from the outside. With only one good eye, I found that it was proving difficult.

Finally I managed to pull the waistband of my boxers down. Even tough my contact was way past rescuing, I decided that I could see well enough for my thrilling encounter to continue. I looked at the guy next to me.

Unfortunately, he was gone, and in his place was a burly mall guard. He took one look at my half-closed eye and the rapidly deflating erection in my hand and frowned.

Now, in the movies, security personnel are notoriously horny and ready for all kinds of fun. I was disheartened to discover that in real life, this is seldom the case. Noting the look in the man's eyes and sensing that somehow trying to explain things to him would probably not help matters any, I beat a hasty retreat from the bathroom. Using my good eye, I managed to make it home, where I collapsed onto the couch.

My day had not gone at all well, and I blamed it all on porn movies. They had promised me a fun-filled existence of sexual freedom, but they had lied. Grabbing an empty box, I moved through the house, gathering up all the videos I could find. When the box was full, I taped it shut and hauled it out to the curb. Dusting off my hands, I went back inside and slammed the door shut on the world of randy men and their empty promises. It was time to come back to reality. Picking up a copy of *Pretty Woman,* I slipped it into the VCR and sat down.

Now there, I thought happily, *is something I can believe in.*

Too Much of a Good Thing

My name is Michael F., and I am a Marthaholic. That's right, I am addicted to Martha Stewart, Goddess of the Art of Living Beautifully. It started innocently enough. I would catch a glimpse of Martha's television show as I was flipping channels. She would be briskly dipping French toast into batter speckled with cinnamon or deftly winding sage leaves into a cunning wreath. *I could do that,* I thought, and I did. It was easy. It made my life a little brighter.

Things went on in this way for a couple of months. I was satisfied by the occasional fix of Martha's helpful hints and her winning smile. Like a freshly baked muffin brimming with ripe blueberries, my encounters with her left me feeling content and happy. But then I found that these small Martha doses just didn't do it for me anymore. I looked at my perfectly poached salmon reclining on its bed of blanched endive, at the cheerful stencils dancing merrily along the edges of my walls, and I wanted more.

So I subscribed to *Martha Stewart Living,* the magazine devoted to my guru and her ways. Each month I had delivered to my mailbox a new installment of the Gospel According to Martha. What a joy it was to rip off the protective plastic bag and stroke the glossy pages with trembling hands before delving into the mysteries awaiting me inside that only She could reveal.

With Martha's guidance I whipped up lemon tarts so light and fluffy, they practically floated out the window. I learned how to refinish and install the claw-foot bathtub I'd always wanted. I tossed together a kitchen herb garden in no time and discovered everything there was to know about Fiestaware, which I began to collect with abandon.

Soon editors began to phone, frenzied when promised manuscripts failed to arrive. "It's almost done," I'd lie, cutting out gingerbread men with my free hand. Worried friends left pleading messages that went unanswered as I experimented with making my own lavender-scented soaps or devising plans for constructing a charming Italianate grotto in the backyard. Finally I unplugged the phone.

Free to immerse myself entirely in Martha's spell, I devoted my every waking moment to her. I copied her personal calendar (helpfully provided in each issue of the magazine), making sure that on the day Martha was ridding her gutters of fall leaves, so was I. On Martha's birthday I built a chicken coop in celebration. I pictured Martha pruning her apple trees, the stray hairs of her carefree bob clinging to her slightly damp brow, and wished for an orchard of my own.

Things finally came to a head the night of my annual Christmas party, which I went forward with only because it was an opportunity to celebrate all things Martha. The handmade invitations, addressed in my finest calligraphy, had gone out two weeks earlier. The fudge was finished, all eighteen kinds individually wrapped in glistening cellophane boxes and decorated with found objects. Presents, all of them handmade according to Martha's own specifications, sat under the tree.

And oh the tree! How it sparkled with the ornaments I'd spun from glass and carved from wood into fantastic shapes! The tiny hand-dipped candles twinkled as I sat sipping my mulled wine and waited for guests to arrive.

By midnight, when no one had come, it hit me. After months of scorning my friends for the company of Martha, they had abandoned me. I looked at the dilled shrimp and plum pudding languishing untouched on the gaily laid table and wept. I was alone on Christmas Eve, and even the spirit of Martha couldn't save me from my despair. I needed professional help.

The next day, after a fitful night spent tossing and turning on the crisp linen sheets that graced my antique sleigh bed, I plugged the phone back in and called the mental health clinic. "Help me," I sobbed when someone picked up. "I can't take it anymore."

Much to my surprise the young woman on the other end quickly referred me to a local chapter of MA — Martha Anonymous. It was held at a nearby address, and there was to be a meeting that very afternoon. Knowing that I needed help to break my Martha addiction, I went.

The room was full. Men and women of all ages sat in folding chairs in front of a podium. Some chatted quietly among themselves. Others sat, hands neatly folded, looking at the floor as though they were picturing in their minds exactly how it would look sanded and refinished in knotty Carolina pine.

A cheerful woman approached me. "Hi," she said. "My name is Anne, and I'm a Marthaholic. Is this your first meeting?"

I nodded. She seemed normal enough. I wondered what her addiction had cost her.

"Thanks for coming," she said. "Have a cookie."

My eyes widened in terror. A cookie! Wasn't that exactly what a Marthaholic would want? I pictured slim fingers of chocolate, delicately beaded with candied violets, or perhaps the thinnest of butter wafers dusted with vanilla sugar.

Anne sensed my alarm. "Don't worry," she said reassuringly. "They're Oreos."

I sat down, sipping reluctantly from a styrofoam cup of bland instant coffee, and Anne began to tell me her story. "It started with the Good Things," she said. "I made little labels for my kids' clothes, covered old shoes with shells and painted them gold, wove ribbon into the edges of my pillowcases. Then it got worse. Soon I was making peach-pie kits for people I barely knew. I emptied the kids' college accounts to pay for terra-cotta planters. I wore gloves so no one could see the marks on my fingers from pushing cloves into orange pomanders. It was sad."

"But you're okay now?" I asked hopefully.

"Oh, no," Anne said gently. "Once a Marthaholic, always a Marthaholic. I still can't walk past a yard sale without breaking into a sweat. But don't worry, we can help."

That afternoon I heard story after story of people whose lives had been devastated by Martha. People who, like me, had been brought to ruin by her promise of enchanted living — losing lovers, jobs, and friends in the process. From them I gained the courage to face my problem, and Anne became my sponsor. We started with the First Step. "I am powerless over Martha," I would repeat to myself every morning as I ate plain cornflakes from a plastic bowl, resisting the craving to improve it with fresh berries and honey from the hive I'd installed out back.

It was hard, but I was determined. Out went all the back issues of *Martha Stewart Living*. I emptied my closets of potpourri, the kitchen drawers of arcane Japanese cooking utensils. I ate store-bought baked goods, gagging on their mass-produced taste. *Arugula* became a forbidden word in my home.

Slowly my system rid itself of Martha's insidious poison. I no longer felt the need to marble every bare inch of wall space. I found that I could indeed eat vegetables that were not grilled over mesquite and doused in raspberry vinegar. After several months of daily phone calls with Anne, I was even able to part with the collection of animal-inspired egg cups I'd collected in my heyday.

I am still not completely cured. Anne was right: Marthaholics never are. I still sometimes pine for a perfectly trained grape arbor, and some mornings I think I won't be able to get out of bed unless I have transplanting pearl onions or creating whimsical picture frames from antique ribbon to look forward to. Holidays are the hardest. But I persevere.

Besides, the other night I was watching PBS and discovered Norm Abrams and *The New Yankee Workshop*. Watching Norm turn ordinary pieces of lumber into beautiful pieces of furniture, I couldn't help but think that the grotto would look so nice with a Shaker table in it.

Adult Education

I did something recently that made me realize how far I've fallen. I became an adult education student.

Time was when I looked upon people who partook of adult education classes as a sort of hopeless breed of, well, completely pathetic losers with nothing else to do but make feeble attempts at learning French or spend six weeks sculpting unidentifiable objects from clay. In my mind they were all forty-somethings named Bernice or George, wore ill-fitting clothes, and smelled faintly of onions. Suddenly keenly aware that they were never going to become ballerinas or stock-car drivers, they would do the next best thing — take a twelve-week seminar on writing a screenplay, which would concern either a lonely housewife trying to fulfill her dreams or a high school baseball star who finds himself twenty years later still employed at the gas station he once saw as a job to tide him over while waiting for major-league clubs to come calling. Seven weeks into the course, stuck at a crucial point in the script's plotting, both Bernice and George would fail to return to class.

But then the catalog came from the local adult education center. At first I tossed it aside derisively, annoyed that I had even been included on a list of people who might have the slightest interest in exploring their dream lives through yoga or attending a series of six minilectures on wines of the world. I wasn't yet thirty. I'd written a dozen successful books. I was, I thought, far too busy living my dreams to go about analyzing them.

A few days later, however, I reached an impassable point in the novel I was working on. Taking a break from it, I sat down and began leafing through the catalog. I thought that seeing what I would become if I failed to finish my book would spur me right through my temporary block. Just looking at the number of "So You Want to Get Published" courses would put the fear of adult ed into me and get me back to work.

And at first it did. I shuddered at the pages listing "Italian Conversation for Beginners" and "Fun With German, Sections I, II, and III" with Mathilde Von Rottgutten, native speaker and author of *Germany: Playground of the Blondes.* I whizzed through the seventeen pages of dance classes (Brazilian, Thai, and two-stepping open to singles) and on past "Quilting a Winning Baby Pillow," "Knitting for Left-handers," and "Tai Chi as Stress Relief."

Where I got stuck was in the cooking section. Now, I love to cook, and I'm pretty good at it. But there are a lot of things I'd like to know how to do that I have just never found the time to learn. Perhaps the pressure of writing full time finally got to me, but for some reason, a cooking class suddenly seemed potentially amusing, even useful. I pictured myself whipping up fantastic dinners for all of my witty friends, where we would sit around contentedly eating and saying very funny things that would have everyone rolling on the floor.

The trick was to select the perfect class. There were some real losers — "French Toast for Cereal Eaters,"

"Bran New Day," and "Salad Roundup," for example. But tucked among the "Barbecue Blowouts" and "Melon Manias" were some things that actually appealed to me. I could hardly believe it as I scanned the listings and found several classes that didn't make me wince. I made a list.

I finally decided on "Sushi!" Not only was it exotic but the Zenlike title, complete with festive exclamation point, reassured me that I would have fun while learning how to create something I'd always wanted to be able to do. As I picked up the phone to make my reservation, I imagined myself deftly handling sharp knives and obscure culinary apparatuses as I sliced up a lovely piece of fish into works of art and served them to amazed acquaintances. Besides, it met for only one night.

I did not, of course, tell anyone that I had sunk to the depths of adult education. Most of my friends are still talking about those Ph. D. s they insist are forthcoming or working diligently toward their master's degrees in folklore or ancient Incan burial rituals. Even their children take ballet and regularly attend postmodern poetry seminars. To admit to signing up for a continuing-ed class would be cause for endless torment. So I kept it to myself.

As the day of my class neared, I found myself growing fearful. What if it turned out to be awful? Did going mean I'd joined the ranks of those who, like my parents, spent their evenings searching for the best fish fry? Worse, what if I couldn't do it? I almost didn't go.

But go I did, and my exploration into the world of ongoing learning almost ended at the door. When I walked into the lobby, I was greeted by the sounds of music. Bad music. Very bad music. It was, I saw by the sign on the wall, a performance of the second-level mandolin class. All thirty-eight of them were sitting on cheerful blue cushions, joyously picking their mandolins and singing "Leaving on a Jet Plane" in several different keys. It was my worst nightmare come true. I suppose I should have just been thankful it wasn't the first-level class.

I would have turned around and fled, but an elderly woman grabbed me and hauled me inside. Apparently this was her job, and she was very good at it. Try as I might, I couldn't pry her wizened little fingers away from my collar. "Now what class are you here for, dear?" she asked, grinning at me over her bifocals.

" 'Sushi!' " I whispered, afraid someone might overhear me.

The woman riffled through a box of index cards. She found the one for my class, checked off my name, and handed me a name tag.

"Fill this out with your name and class, and wear it at all times," she said. "We like to be friendly around here."

I did not feel at all friendly, but being rather intimidated by matronly women wearing running shoes and CLINTON/GORE T-shirts, I obliged. I peeled off the back and stuck the MIKE/SUSHI badge to my chest. The woman smiled again.

"Good," she said. "Now go right through that door. Your class is in the third room on the right."

I waded through the sea of warbling mandolin players and pushed open the door. Thankful to be free of the awful singing, I started down the hall. It reminded me of being in third grade, where everything is painted the same peculiar shade of green and trying to find homeroom produces waves of nausea. I found what I thought was the right door and went in. A group of thirteen people stared at me. I glanced at the nearest name tag. ELISE/PAST-LIFE REGRESSION it read. I excused myself. I have enough trouble with this life.

Eventually I found the correct room and went in. Sitting around a table were seven other people sporting badges bearing their names — TREVOR/SUSHI, MITZI/SUSHI, SHANIQUA/SUSHI, and so on. I took a seat next to SASHA/SUSHI because I liked the sound of it. Sasha, like almost everyone else in the room except myself and ELIZABETH/SUSHI, who looked to be about sixteen and appeared to be sporting a hat of her own design, was at least sixty-seven years old. She had an enormous quantity of white hair, which she wore in two long braids.

"Hi," I said, remembering that I was supposed to be friendly. "I like your necklace." Sasha was wearing a peculiar-looking piece around her neck.

"Thanks," she said brightly. "I made it in my last class — 'Body as Art.' It's a replica of my vagina in bronze."

I stared at her, not knowing what one was supposed to say when forced to comment on a new acquaintance's privates. She looked so hopeful, like my dog when he's actually fetched the stick and wants my praise. "Well," I said finally. "It's certainly shiny."

Sasha beamed. "I love adult ed, don't you?"

"This is my first class," I said.

"A virgin!" Sasha yelped, a little more loudly than I would have liked. The other students looked over at me. I waved tentatively, still trying to be friendly, as I thought about strangling Sasha with her vagina.

Thankfully I was saved by the arrival of the instructor. I was a little bit surprised to see that he was about as Japanese as I am — which is not at all — and was sporting a Red Sox T-shirt and Bermuda shorts. "Good evening," he said. "My name is Morty Rosenblum, and I'm your instructor."

I raised my hand. "Are you a sushi chef?" I asked.

Morty gave me a withering look. "No," he said. "But I spent time in Japan as an exchange student."

While I was immediately dubious, this answer seemed to satisfy the other students, all of whom nodded and smiled at Morty and at one another. We then went around the table and introduced ourselves while Morty spent a lot of time shuffling some papers back and forth. As I'd expected, everyone else in the class had taken at least three other continuing-ed courses, sometimes more than once. ELIZABETH/SUSHI had taken "Motorcycle Repair and Maintenance" six times.

After these pleasantries, the class began in earnest. Things seemed to pick up as Morty introduced us to the various pieces of equipment we would need to make flawless sushi. We passed around a *makisu* (bamboo rolling mat), *kijakushi* (rice paddle), *hashi* (chopsticks), and other intriguing items, the names of which Morty read from a piece of paper and which I wrote on the back of an envelope I found in my backpack. The other students diligently wrote everything down in little notebooks.

We were then instructed in the centuries-old art of making sushi rice. Apparently in Japan the making of sushi rice is a sacred event, second only to the making of Godzilla movies in its attention to detail. It involves heating the rice to exact temperatures, adding just the right amount of vinegar, turning it frequently with a specially designed kijakushi handed down from generation to generation, and watching it every single second so that it comes out the desired consistency with every grain going in the same direction. Years are spent teaching would-be itamae (sushi chefs) how to make rice, and poor sushi rice is a shame no itamae can bear.

Luckily for those of us without several decades to spend stirring and paddling, Morty suggested that Uncle Ben's with a splash of rice vinegar would do just fine, thus saving us years of toil and resulting in perfect rice in ten minutes every time.

We then moved on to what most people think of when they think of sushi — raw fish. Morty produced a nice length of fresh tuna and proceeded to show us how to slice it up into tender morsels fit for any tsu (sushi lover). He then presented us each with a small piece of our own and told us to go to it. I watched as SASHA/SUSHI picked up her knife and quickly turned her tuna into five glistening pieces of equal thickness and length. Reaching into the rice pot, she deftly formed five fingers (as the lengths of compressed rice are called, we learned) of perfect size and laid her tuna cross them without a problem.

Spurred on by her success, I tackled my piece of tuna. Ten minutes later I had one ragged-looking rectangle of fish and a pile of scraps. Undaunted, I reached into the rice bowl and pulled out a fistful. This I turned into five blobs reminiscent of my first encounters with Play-Doh in kindergarten. I dumped my fish pieces on top and looked at it. It was sad.

"Maybe it will look better with some pickled ginger on it," SASHA/SUSHI said, her vagina tinkling against her chest.

I had even worse luck with rolled sushi. Try as I might, my pieces of nori (seaweed) refused to cooperate, and my rolls ended up looking like some kind of amputated limb from a leprous sea creature, the cucumber strips and imitation crab spilling out like so much offal onto the plate. SASHA/SUSHI peered over her pyramid of perfectly rolled pieces and gave me a sympathetic smile.

My adventure into adult ed was beginning to wear on me. Everyone else seemed to be having a good time, slicing up yellowtail and rolling bits of eel into fantastical shapes. Their knives flew, their bamboo mats whispered, and out came sushi fit for even the most discriminating gourmand.

My last chance came with hand rolls. Essentially a hand roll is a sushi ice cream cone. You simply roll up a piece of nori, drop some rice and fish into it, and there you are. Foolproof. I was determined to make one. Looking out of the corner of my eye to see what SASHA/SUSHI was doing, I snatched up my seaweed, formed a cone, and filled it slowly with its fish contents. I did everything she did, down to the last folding of the nori to keep it all together. When I was done, I laid it on the plate and gazed upon it with pride.

Approximately three seconds later, it fell apart. The rice spilled out like an avalanche, the fish slipping down it like some fleshy sled gone out of control until it coasted to a stop at the side of the plate next to the lumpy blob of wasabi (horseradish paste) I'd stuck there. I wanted to cry.

Morty walked around the classroom, observing our accomplishments. He gave each student little pieces of advice to think about the next time she or he delighted in the art of sushi. When he came to me, he looked at the pile of rice and fish on my plate and patted me on the back. "I hear two-stepping is fun," he said consolingly.

SASHA/SUSHI offered me a ride home on the back of her moped, but I declined. I went home that night alone and dejected, an adult-education failure. All I had to show for my effort was an old envelope with lists of arcane Japanese sushi terms and a fish stain on it. *What will I ever do with this?* I thought, crumpling it up.

I flipped on my computer and opened the file with my novel in it. I was on page 173 and still hadn't broken through the barrier that had caused my initial foray into the realm of ongoing learning.

I typed for a while but with no success. The story just wouldn't come. Glancing over at the desk, I saw the course catalog lying where I'd left it next to the phone. I picked it up and turned to the writing classes.

Dyke the Halls

I have always had a close group of lesbian friends, so having the girls over for a little Christmas get-together seemed like a fine notion. Perhaps encouraged by faulty memories of my own childhood holidays, one day I decided to invite some of them to come help me select and decorate a tree. We would, I thought, go out and cut one of the many pines that grew wild on the land around my house. Then, warmed by goodwill and vast quantities of hot chocolate, we would trim it while listening to carols and eating homemade cookies, perhaps even with green and red sprinkles on top. It would all be wildly fun and a wonderful way to celebrate with our extended gay family before the annual horror of going home to our real ones. Really, it seemed like a good idea at the time.

The first sign of trouble came with the first telephone call, made to my friend Willow.

"Christmas is an Anglo-patriarchal holiday that bastardizes traditional goddess-worship celebrations," she said after I asked her.

"I always thought it was about presents and singing and elves," I said.

"Furthermore," continued Willow grimly, "the whole Judeo-Christian concept of the season is a reprehensible fallacy that completely minimizes the spiritual belief systems of other cultures. All of those horrible Nativity scenes that pop up all over shopping malls across America — they're just representations of what the church would like us to think Christmas is."

"But the presents..." I countered.

"I just can't condone participating in that kind of perpetuation," said Willow. "I mean, this whole celebration — which really you should call 'Yule' anyway — is supposed to be about the coming of the horned god and the cold winter months, not about some fat white man in a suit abusing endangered animals by making them pull a sleigh, which is really probably far too heavy for them anyway."

"Okay, so it's a Yule celebration," I said.

"But the point I'm trying—"

"We're having cheesecake," I said.

Willow said she'd be there by 6.

Next on my list was Rachel. She had just finished meditating and seemed to be in a good mood. I took this as a positive sign. "I'm having a Christ...er...Yule party," I said warmly. "I was hoping you'd come."

"I'm Jewish," she said. "We don't do Yule. Christmas either."

I sighed. "What do you do?"

"Nothing," Rachel said. "Well, there's Hanukkah, but I find the whole thing ridiculous. People rushing all over buying crap no one wants just because they feel bad that their kids don't get to visit Santa. It just makes me crazy."

She was warming up for a lecture, so I cut her off. "Look," I said, "this isn't about presents. We're just getting together, and it happens to be Yule or Christmas or some damn thing. I haven't seen you in a month. Are you coming or not?"

"Well, if you're going to make me feel guilty about it, I guess I have to."

I took that as a yes and told her what time to be there.

Anne was the last person to call. Prepared by my encounters with Willow and Rachel, I told Anne I was having a holiday party, which I would like her to participate in so that we could nondenominationally celebrate nothing and have a good time communing in one another's company.

"Fine," she said.

"Fine?"

"Yes, fine. What did you expect me to say?"

"Um, I don't know."

"I'll be there," she finished, adding before hanging up, "I'll bring my new girlfriend." So excited was I by her smooth acceptance that I failed to register the last part of her sentence. I would live to regret it.

The day of the festivities dawned cold and gray. By noon a light snow was falling, the perfect backdrop for what I hoped would be a pleasant evening with my friends. As the hour neared, I made the last batches of cookies and set them out to cool. Everything was ready, and all I needed was the guests. I began to think happy thoughts. I put on a Windham Hill *Solstice* sampler album, pleased that it contained no religious connotations whatsoever but still sounded wintry.

They all arrived simultaneously, bustling into the house like a pack of cats caught in the rain and trying desperately to get out. "It's snowing," Rachel said glumly. "It's practically a blizzard."

Willow handed me a package wrapped in brown paper and tied with twine. "Here," she said. "It's a candle to burn for Yule. It brings happiness."

"I thought we weren't giving presents," Rachel said defensively. "I didn't bring anything because you said—"

"It's not a present," I said hurriedly. "It's a...a...a ceremonial object."

"I thought we weren't doing anything religious," Rachel started again but was cut off by Anne, who entered accompanied by a tall, thin woman wearing an Army surplus jacket and John Lennon glasses.

"This is Hannah," she said. "We met at the co-op."

Thankful for the distraction, I picked up a plate of cookies. "Nice to meet you," I said. "Would you care for a gingerbread boy?"

"Person," said Hannah.

I looked at her blankly. "Gingerbread *person*," she repeated. "Not *boy*. Do they have sugar, butter, or eggs in them."

"Yes, yes, and yes," I said. "Why?"

"I don't eat anything with animal products or processed sweeteners. No wheat, either."

I glared at Anne over Hannah's shoulder. "Would you like some mulled wine then?"

"I don't drink alcohol," Hannah said. "But never mind. I brought my own soy milk and some rice cakes." She pulled a bag from her oversize Guatemalan peasant's pouch and proceeded to snack.

Thankfully no one else had any qualms about sugar or fat, and we all dived into the piles of cookies. After a half hour or so of munching and chatting, I announced that it was time to go get the tree.

"Tree?" Rachel said, her mouth overflowing with chocolate chip–macadamia nut crunchies. "You didn't say anything about a tree."

"I forgot," I said. "We're going to get a tree." I looked over at Willow, who seemed to be chanting under her breath. "It's a Yule tree."

"Oy," said Rachel, heaving herself out of her chair. "The things you goys do."

Eventually I got everyone dressed and out into the yard. After a short trek through the now-snowy woods, we came to the tree I'd preselected earlier in the week and tied with a red bow so I could find it again. "Here it is," I said proudly. "The Yule tree."

"You're going to cut down a tree?" said Hannah. "A living tree?"

I smiled at her, gritting my teeth. "Yes," I said evenly. "Why?"

Hannah snorted. "Well, go right ahead. But what with the destruction of the rain forests in South America and all, I'd think maybe you'd want to leave this tree in peace."

I produced the handsaw from the bag I was carrying. "I'm sure this one tree won't cause the ozone layer to instantly evaporate," I said, waving the saw menacingly in Hannah's direction.

"She's right," said Willow. "I mean, you didn't tell me you were going to cut down a real tree or anything."

I looked at her through squinted eyes. "Just where did you think Yule trees came from?" I asked. "Do you think the Yule people or goddess worshipers or whatever they were made them out of old newspapers?"

"At least say a prayer to its spirit," Willow insisted. "Really, if you're going to kill it and all, the least you can do is tell it you're sorry. You owe it something."

We all joined hands around the tree. I stared at it, wishing it would just fall over on its own.

Everyone was waiting for me to say something. I cleared my throat. "Dear tree," I said, feeling like the biggest ass on earth, "thank you for giving your life that we might have a joyous Yule season."

I looked over at Willow. "Happy?"

She nodded. I picked up the saw and knelt beneath the tree. I put the edge of the saw against the trunk, only to hear Willow and Hannah break out in violent weeping.

"Okay," I said, standing up. "Everyone into the Volvo."

We piled into the car and drove to the tree stand set up at the end of town. My Christmas/Yule/holiday celebration was turning into one gigantic nightmare, but I was determined to have a good time. We all got out and started to walk through the aisles of trees, searching for the perfect specimen. Although Willow still sniffled a little as she ran her hands over the branches of the fallen trees, she behaved herself.

After looking at every single tree in the entire place, we were finally able to select one that looked decent. Although Hannah said she was sure it was some kind of endangered fir and threatened to turn the owner of the place over to the Sierra Club, Greenpeace, and Robert Redford, I plunked down $45 and tied the hapless tree to the roof of the car. Everyone got back in, and we went home.

With a minor amount of fuss, we got the tree into its stand and settled into a corner of the living room, where it seemed a little overwhelmed. I hauled out a box of ornaments, and we set to work trimming it. I put Rachel in charge of stringing lights, Anne was responsible for hanging balls, and Willow and Hannah volunteered for tinsel detail because it involved the least amount of physical contact with what they insisted on calling "the wounded soul." Cookies were eaten and drinks were drunk, and soon things were humming right along. At least for five minutes.

The lights were the first problem. I should have been watching Rachel more carefully or at least been suspicious when I heard her cackle every few minutes as she bustled around the tree. "There we are!" she said triumphantly, plugging them in so the room filled with merry color. The lights were on the tree, all right, and for once they all worked. But they were arranged in a strange pattern that defied explanation.

"What did you do?" I asked. "It looks funny."

"I arranged them in the shape of a vulva," she said proudly. "See how the labia wrap around the sides? Isn't it great?"

I sighed. "It's lovely," I said. "Let's just hang the decorations."

"I don't know about these," Anne said, looking doubtfully at my box of ornaments. She held up a frosted glass ball in one hand and a hand-blown icicle in the other. "How come these are all phallic-oriented? Don't you have any pink triangles or labryses or busts of Gertrude Stein?"

"Pretend the balls are breasts," I said. "And the angels are drag queens from the Stonewall Riots."

Anne was skeptical, but she went to work, hanging balls and icicles and angels with abandon until she'd gone through the entire box. "Are there more?" she asked.

"In the guest-room closet," I said, busy trying to arrange holly on the mantel. "Top shelf."

Anne disappeared. I stood looking at the tree, munching on a cookie. "This hasn't been so bad after all," I said to Rachel, who was trying to get a red light to line up with where a clitoris should be.

All of a sudden, Anne ran back into the room crying. She grabbed her coat and headed out the door. "What's wrong?" I asked her.

She turned around. "Willow is in the guest room teaching Hannah the basics of tantric yoga!" she sobbed before getting into her Subaru and pulling out of the driveway.

A moment later Hannah and Willow appeared in the doorway, looking slightly flushed. "Hey, what's going on?" Willow asked.

"Anne saw you two playing 'O Come All Ye Faithful,' " I said. "Now she's gone."

"Oh, shit," said Hannah. "She still has my WOMYN FOR A FREE TIBET T-shirt in her trunk."

Willow snatched up her coat and left, followed closely by Hannah, who ran down the driveway yelling "Wait, I need a ride!" her Birkenstocks making patterns in the snow.

I shut the door and turned to Rachel. "Well, that was fun!" she said. "Now, shall we hang this tinsel or not?"

I grabbed a handful and flung it at the tree, where it landed and hung like some cheap stripper's bedraggled fright wig, reflecting the changing colors of the lights as the vulva twinkled gaily. I sank into a chair and moaned.

On the table cheesecake sat untouched, while the wine mulled on in silence.

"Look on the bright side," Rachel said, unwrapping Willow's Yule candle and lighting it. "There's always New Year's."

Taking the Credit

I read somewhere the other day that the average American owes $3,450 in credit card bills. That information alone is unsettling. Then, using all kinds of charts and formulas, the article went on to prove that if the original debt were paid off using only the minimum payment due each month, it would take more than thirty years and require almost $6,000 in finance charges to completely pay it off. In other words, you would have paid for whatever it was you bought almost two times over. So those towels you got for 15 percent off at the Macy's white sale really ended up costing you $128. 53. Did you really need them that badly?

In the '70s, when credit cards first started to become really popular, I would stand in line with my father and listen to him rant and rave about how long it was taking to check out because someone ahead of us had decided to use Visa. In those days paying with plastic required a prolonged procedure involving eighteen slips of carbon paper, a call to get the card number approved, and sometimes even a little dance to invoke the finance spirits, who would, if provoked, cause the receipt machine to jam. I recall quite vividly the grumbling and foot tapping that ensued whenever anyone dared utter the terrible words, "I'd like to charge that, please." My father said it was just a fad and would never last. He said the same thing about men wearing earrings.

Now, of course, you can't leave the house without plastic. In my wallet are two credit cards (American Express and Visa), an electronic library card, a card to use at the supermarket to get surprise bargains, a card for making telephone calls, a card for renting movies at the video store, a card that gets me a discount at the vitamin store, and a bank card that allows me to do amazing things at ATM machines and that also somehow functions as a MasterCard. I haven't touched actual cash in months. The money just flows in and out of my account electronically, like a tide of cybernetic krill being swallowed up and regurgitated by a gigantic computerized whale.

And I'm fairly streamlined. I have friends who have dozens of credit cards, store cards, frequent-flier cards, gas cards, and bank cards. Their accumulated debt is in the tens of thousands, yet they never seem to worry. They just keep transferring balances from one card to another, gaining an extra sixty days before payments are due again. On day fifty-nine, they simply switch again, generally to a card with lower interest. When one card turns its weary back and says, "Not tonight," there's always another one waiting with open arms.

Not me. I've learned my lesson the hard way. For years I had only one credit card — American Express ("Member Since 1989"). The plain old green card. I got it when I got my first job. I trusted it because, since the balance has to be paid every month, I knew I wouldn't go overboard. And this worked very well for a long time.

I bought what I needed; I paid it off. Signing the receipts at restaurants or in stores, I felt very grown up and responsible.

But after a few months of happy bliss, the onslaught began. As soon as I got my American Express card, others began wooing me. All of a sudden a plain old credit card wasn't good enough. The really cool cards didn't just pay for things; they gave you stuff too. Seemingly every day another offer came in: free flight miles for every dollar spent, a percentage donated to worthy causes, "bonus credits" that could be traded in for gifts, even cash back at the end of the year. The more I bought, the more I earned. (That logic escapes me now, but at the time I fell for it.) In the face of such temptations, my little green AmEx card seemed pale and weak.

I called American Express. "Why can't my card earn me free car rentals?" I demanded. "Why does it just sit there while the other cards do magical tricks and cough up goodies left and right?"

The operator was cheerful. "What you need," she said, "is the Gold Card."

Until then I had no idea such a thing existed. A Gold Card. It sounded so regal. So chic. So much better than a boring old green card. Why, it was even capitalized, while the green card, like some obscure East Village poet, had to be content with going about lowercased. I signed up on the spot.

My Gold Card came a few days later, sealed in a smart-looking pouch and stamped with an official-looking gold seal. I even had to go sign for it at the post office, which made it all the more thrilling. Once home, I tore open the pouch and gazed at my new treasure. When I moved it around in the light, it sparkled promisingly.

According to the booklet that was enclosed with the card, my upgrade came with all kinds of features I would soon find indispensable. I could, for example, purchase $100,000 worth of travel insurance just by asking for it. Or I could take advantage of the many holiday travel packages put together on a regular basis by the thoughtful folks at American Express, who had reserved a cabin in Montana just for me. I was assured that holders of the ordinary old green card had no such perks and were a decidedly inferior lot. They, of course, weren't paying $75 a year either, but I didn't dwell on that for more than a moment. It seemed a small price to pay for a cabin in Montana.

I couldn't wait to use my Gold Card, so I took my friend Katherine out to dinner. When it came time to pay, I whipped out my shiny new card and placed it gently on the table. "Where'd you get that?" Katherine asked.

"They gave it to me," I said. "All I had to do was ask. Isn't it pretty?"

"But you make no money," she said, shocked. "I thought the Gold Card was for all of those business majors we hated in college, the ones with jobs on Wall Street now."

"They said my credit rating was superb," I answered proudly.

Now, Katherine wasn't as off the mark as you might think. It used to be that things like Gold Cards and $15,000 credit limits were reserved for people who actually made enough money to buy things worth $15,000. Not anymore. These days a mere child can get a $20,000 limit simply by asking for it. In fact, the deeper into debt you go, the higher they raise your limit. When my friend Jesse surpassed his $12,500 Visa limit, they sent him a cheese log and a $5,000 upgrade.

I was to find out just how this worked about a year later. I had been happily using my Gold Card for everything. I had even   once — taken advantage of what the company cryptically referred to as my "membership privileges," a term that implied all manner of clandestine activity, like secret handshakes and meeting strange men on dark corners to exchange packages. I had used my card to purchase tickets to an Indigo Girls concert, where I was assured that I would have the absolute best seats at Radio City Music Hall, reserved especially for people who, like me, were good enough to have been given the Gold Card.

The night of the show, I arrived and found my seats. They were very good indeed. Very near the stage. But they weren't the best. In front of me a herd of teenage girls sat chatting, waiting for the show to begin. Certain that they couldn't possibly have Gold Cards of their own, I casually tapped one on the shoulder and asked where she had gotten her tickets.

"Oh," she said, "my father has an American Express Platinum Card."

I felt as though I'd been slapped. A Platinum Card? Until then I'd assumed that a Gold Card was the pinnacle of success. I thought I'd arrived. Now, if the girl was to be believed, I discovered that I still had a ways to go. Distressed, I was completely unable to enjoy the show, even when Amy and Emily encouraged the audience to sing along on the chorus of "Least Complicated." I tried, but my heart just wasn't in it.

For weeks I was disconsolate. Then out of the blue, an envelope arrived in the mail. At first I thought it was a wedding invitation because it was very thick and hand-addressed in fine calligraphy. Then I noticed the American Express address on the back. Opening it, I pulled out an engraved card. "You are cordially invited," it said on the outside. Inside it went on to inform me that "in the next few days you will be receiving a special invitation." It didn't say to what.

The next few days were tense ones as I waited expectantly to see what was coming. Finally, a large vellum envelope arrived. Inside was another engraved invitation. "Because you are in the top 1% of the financial elite," it read, "we are extending to you our greatest honor."

It was, remarkably, an invitation to accept the Platinum Card. Along with the invitation was a book — an actual book — outlining all the pleasures the Platinum Card could bring me if I "choose to accept this wonderful distinction." The whole package was more extensive than any of the college prospectuses I'd received in high school.

"You, a Platinum Card?" my roommate said, looking over my shoulder as I read. "What did you make last year, $20,000 or something?"

"It doesn't matter," I said, caressing the soft leather cover of *The Guidebook to the Platinum Card*. "I'm one of the financial elite."

I spent all night reading the book. I discovered, among other things, that owning the card would give me guaranteed reservations to the world's trendiest restaurants. Never mind that an evening out for me usually involved mediocre Indian food and a frozen yogurt —

now I had my very own table at the Four Seasons. Not only that, but Platinum Card owners could get, with no fuss whatsoever, tickets to any show in any city, just by calling one easy-to-remember phone number. It was all too good to be true, especially for a little boy from Barneveld, New York.

The thing that finally hooked me, however, wasn't the guaranteed seating or the marvelous tickets. It was the "Personal Assistant" service. According to the book, if I were to become a Platinum Card owner, the entire American Express company was at my disposal should I ever need help. Say, for example, I was on a business trip and feeling a little tense. All I had to do was call American Express and within minutes a masseur would be at my door, ready to knead the worry away. Or suppose I required a unique and thoughtful gift for a client or loved one. One call to AmEx and a personal shopper would scour the world's best shops for a one-of-a-kind item, wrap it, and send it by overnight mail, along with a personally written card bearing my name.

How could I pass up such a wonderful thing? I pictured myself in a strange city — Singapore, perhaps — and discovering that I'd just left my briefcase with my new novel in it in the backseat of the cab that was speeding away. Not to worry. Stepping into the lobby of my hotel (four-star, of course), I would pick up the phone and dial 1-800-PLAT-CARD. A courteous employee would pick up on the first ring. After hearing my story, she would immediately dispatch a young man to comb the city for my missing briefcase while I repaired to the finest restaurant in town and enjoyed a lovely dinner. Upon my return to the hotel, my briefcase would be waiting for me at the desk. Not only would my manu-

script be safely in my hands once more but my thoughtful personal assistant would have taken the time to copy-
edit it for me and rewrite the ending, which had been
troubling me on the flight over.

Ignoring the small print about the $300-a-year
membership fee, I returned my RSVP card and waited.
The card arrived a week later, ensconced in a blue vel-
vet box embossed with a platinum AmEx logo. After
washing my hands, I carefully pried off the lid and
beheld my new card in all its glory. Surely Mary herself
had not beheld the baby Jesus with quite the same awe.
It was lovely, bearing a gentle silver finish with my own
name stamped in sharp relief. I cradled it in my hands
and sighed.

If I'd been excited about using my Gold Card, I was
orgasmic over the Platinum Card. Once again I took
Katherine to dinner. This time we went to a restaurant
with a two-month wait for tables.

"How'd you get reservations?" she asked, examining
the real silver place settings. "Have you been sleeping
with a waiter again?"

"No," I said casually, sliding the Platinum Card out of
my wallet. "I just used this."

Katherine's eyes went wide. "Good lord!" she whispered. "Is it real?"

"Yup," I said. "Want to touch it?"

Over the next month, I used my Platinum Card
often and well. Every time I looked at it, I got a warm
feeling inside. Whenever I handed it to a sales clerk or
waiter, I beamed with pride. Then the bill came. All
$2,326.78 of it. I opened the envelope (which disap-
pointingly was not vellum but the same plain old paper
they sent the green card bills in) and nearly fainted. I

couldn't believe things had gotten so out of control. And I'd never even used the masseur or the personal assistant!

In the end, I never did use them. That one bill was enough to knock some sense into me. After taking out a cash advance from another card (at 19. 8 percent interest) to pay off AmEx, I called and canceled my Platinum account.

"Just give me back the green card," I said sadly.

"The green card?" the operator replied incredulously. "You're giving up the Platinum Card for the green card? But we're offering Platinum members box seats for the Rangers' games for only $4,000."

For a moment I was tempted. Then I remembered my 19.8 percent interest. "No, thanks," I said, trying not to cry.

It took me two years to finally pay off the cash advance. With interest, my little Platinum Card party ended up costing me $3,342.18. Now I'm back to the green card, which is fine with me. I'm still so shaken I can barely take it out of my wallet without weeping. But I still have that Platinum Card, resting in its little blue velvet box. And sometimes, when I'm feeling down, I take it out and remember a time when I was one of the financial elite.

The Nonwriting Life

Writers who claim they've wanted to write since the age of six and would die if they couldn't write are pathological liars.

I hate writing. In fact, I will do almost anything to avoid doing it, and actually getting me to produce something is no less a miracle than it must have been to construct the hanging gardens at Babylon. If it wasn't for the simple fact that I am totally unemployable in any other capacity, I probably wouldn't write at all. And if someone were to offer me a vast sum of cash to stop, I would. Why Joe Eszterhas, the screenwriter of such classics as *Showgirls* and *Basic Instinct,* and the highest-paid writer in Hollywood, refuses to make the same concession, I cannot understand. He's probably written since he was six.

Discovering this about me amazes people who know that I have made a living as a writer for several years now. This is because people have interesting ideas about writers. Most think we spring from our beds each morning and leap to the keyboard to get down all the fresh ideas that have been birthed in the subconscious while we sleep. They envision us spending joyous days at the computer creating marvelous new worlds and turning out witty phrases left and right until, breathless from the act of creation and weak from forgetting to eat, we repair to the kitchen for a light snack of leftover sushi before settling down to watch something stimulating on PBS.

I do know writers like that, but they are not to be trusted, and I do not speak to them. My own life, and that of most full-time writers I know, is far less glamorous. How books are written remains a mystery I do not fully understand, even though I have produced close to two dozen of them. I know only that, in my case, they generally are pieced together in fits of activity that come between extended periods of not doing anything at all.

Take, for instance, this past Tuesday, which is fairly representative of most of my days. At 5:30 I got up and, after stumbling about in the dark trying to find my clothes, took Roger, my black lab, to the park for a swim and a run with his friends. Now lest you think my getting up at this early hour is an admirable display of affection for my loyal pet, I should explain that we do this because predawn is the only time the park is not overrun by joggers and fishermen, two groups of people whom neither Roger nor I need added to our morning experience. It also means I don't have to make elaborate excuses for going to bed at 8:30 in the evening and refusing to have dinner with people I don't like.

When we returned several hours later, Roger enjoyed a leisurely breakfast on the porch while I ate potato chips and Lotsa Lemon yogurt and wondered why all the geraniums were yellowing. I then spent from 8:30 until 9 examining the plants and trying to cheer them up, unsuccessfully, by spritzing them with a mixture of fish meal and bottled water. What I was really doing was not working on the book that I'd promised my editor would be on her desk by Friday but that in truth I had not even begun to write.

At 9 o'clock I turned on *Oprah,* which I watch because my agent says that authors who appear on her show make million of dollars, and I figure tuning in each day will give me some tips on how to write books Oprah likes. On this particular morning, the guest happened to be Toni Morrison. I had sort of been hoping for Zack, a seventy-pound two-year-old who had been making the talk-show rounds of late, but I settled for what I could get. Besides, it was literary and was therefore not a waste of time. Everything went well until Oprah asked what Toni liked best about being a writer. "Oh, I don't think I can call myself a writer," Morrison said. "I don't think anyone can make a living by writing these days. It's just too hard."

I turned off the TV. Toni Morrison has several best-selling novels and a Nobel Prize to her credit, and she still won't call herself a writer. I don't even have a savings account. And I've written more books than she has. Surely it was a sign that I should just stop. I started to scan the help-wanted ads but decided it was too much effort because they weren't listed alphabetically.

From 10 to 11, I checked my E-mail, none of which was important but all of which was deeply fascinating in comparison to trying to write something. I then answered it all, writing thoughtful and incisive responses in the event that a century from now someone will want to know what I had to say about things. Having sent it, I opened WordPerfect and began to look through all of my files, deciding that it was a wonderful opportunity to clear things out and, thus newly organized, begin my writing work with a fresh outlook.

At 1:30, while I was deeply engrossed in reading a self-help book on visualizing success (deleting the files had become boring when I realized there was nothing new since the last time I'd cleaned them out), the phone rang. Visualizing someone calling with an offer of cash, I picked it up. Still, ever wary that it might be a disgruntled editor, I disguised my voice.

"Hello?" I said gruffly, adopting a slightly irritated tone, as though interrupted in the middle of composing something utterly brilliant.

"Relax, it's me," said my friend Katherine. She is a writer too and is almost as good at avoiding actually writing as I am.

"What are you doing?" I asked, pleased to have something to rescue me from almost working. Since Katherine had called me, I had the passive-aggressive advantage of having her to blame later for my unproductive day.

"Nothing," she said flatly. "I got up at noon and watched a *Murphy Brown* rerun. I was thinking about going to the library, but I'm too tired."

Being tired is a central quality of all full-time writers. I cannot recall the last day on which I did not have a nap.

"Maybe you should write something," I suggested lightly. I was hoping Katherine might actually believe for a moment that I was really working.

"Right," said Katherine instantly. "When's the last time you wrote something?"

I thought about that. "I handed a manuscript in at the beginning of February," I said. "A novel. Rent was due."

Katherine was impressed. "I haven't handed anything in for months," she said. "In fact, I forget what it is I'm supposed to be working on."

"The article about lesbians in China," I reminded her. While we seldom do any of our own work, writers can always remember the details of what our friends are not working on. That way we always know who would be ahead if anything were actually written.

"Oh, yeah," she said sleepily. "That's been due for weeks."

I sighed. "You know, I wish I had something interesting to work on," I said. "That would make it so much easier to be motivated."

"You have three books under contract," Katherine said.

"But none of them are interesting," I complained. "I didn't think they'd actually buy them when I sent in the proposals. I just needed to feel like I was doing something."

"Just write them," Katherine said. "What about your column?"

I needed to change the subject. Being reminded of everything I wasn't writing was making me tense. "Do you think Joyce Carol Oates and Stephen King have conversations like this?" I asked.

"Probably," said Katherine. "I bet she eats Oreos all morning and then calls him to see what he's doing."

"And he's sitting there playing solitaire on his Mac," I added. It made me feel better to imagine writers more famous than myself sitting around not writing too.

Katherine and I talked for a long time about not writing and about what Joyce and Stephen were doing. By the time we were done, we had them engaged in trying to create a stained-glass effect on their office windows while avoiding finishing first drafts of their new books, something Katherine and I had actually done a few years back. Then I looked at the clock. It was 3 o'clock, time for Roger's walk. I said good-bye to Katherine and hung up.

After Roger's walk, I gathered the mail and scanned it hopefully for (1) letters from publishers with checks, (2) letters from readers with kind words and/or checks, and (3) magazines that would give me something to do for the rest of the afternoon. Sadly, there were no checks or kind letters, but there was a new issue of *Entertainment Weekly*. Grabbing the cookies from the kitchen, I sat on the porch and started to read while Roger dozed in the sun. It would, I thought, help me relax for all the writing I would not do later in the afternoon.

About halfway through the magazine, I came across an article about a young writer, who was not Joe Eszterhas, who had just been paid $2 million for a script that apparently featured neither plot nor characters. I snatched up the phone and speed-dialed Katherine's number. She picked up immediately, using the same mock-annoyed tone I had adopted earlier.

"It's me," I said. "Listen to this." I read her the article. When I was done, I sighed. "It's not fair," I said plaintively. "I could have written that."

Men and Other
Obstacles to Happiness

How Alec Baldwin Ruined My Life

I'm saving myself for marriage. My mother would be so proud. Unfortunately, there's one small problem: The man of my dreams is taken, and I'm not getting any younger waiting around for him. Yes, the world is a sorry place indeed. Crime is rampant. Children can't read. People are homeless. It's enough to make any sympathetic person weep for days. But while these things are indeed terrible, they are not the worst things about the world, not by a long shot. No, the worst thing is that Alec Baldwin is married, and not to me.

Don't laugh. This is a serious issue. You see, Alec was my first and only real love. Ever since I was seventeen and saw him on television in the homo-oriented TV mini-series *Dress Gray,* I've known I would marry him. From the moment he slipped off his attractive officer's uniform and I saw the dark line of hair peeking out over the edge of his crisp white T-shirt, I was hooked. Then there were the eyes, so blue and inviting. The secretive smile. And the voice. So sensual. So masculine. I could just imagine how it would sound whispering my name as he slipped into bed and put his arm around me. After the scene in which he lowers himself into a hot bath, I was a believer in love at first sight.

Once I'd found my man, I set about getting ready for him. Having grown up with two older sisters whose primary objective in life was getting married as quickly as humanly possible, I knew how it was done. I prepared a hope chest, filled with everything my man could desire. I embroidered little linen guest towels with my new initials. I collected flatware in an appealing design and chose a china pattern that was both homey and elegant. I loaded up on sheets I knew Alec would look the most handsome reclining on in his white boxer shorts on our honeymoon night.

Then I waited. I knew that if I was patient, Alec would come. No matter that we moved in two different worlds. I had fate and little linen guest towels on my side. In the meantime, I saw all of his movies — *The Alamo: Thirteen Days to Glory, Beetlejuice, Married to the Mob, She's Having a Baby, Working Girl, Talk Radio,* and even *Forever, Lulu.* No matter how brief Alec's appearances in a film, in my eyes he was the star. *Great Balls of Fire. The Hunt for Red October. Miami Blues.* With each movie, my love for Alec deepened. I sat in the audience, eating popcorn and wishing I could reach out to pat his thigh and tell him how magnificent he was on screen, even in the smallest roles.

Then came *The Marrying Man.* Oh, sure, I admit that I'd heard all the stories about his off-the-set romance with costar Kim Basinger. I'd secretly read the tabloids while waiting in line at the supermarket and seen the pictures of them kissing. But I knew it was just hype, a carefully orchestrated publicity stunt to boost the buzz around what was, with the obvious exception of Alec, a terrible film. I didn't sense any real danger. After all, surely Alec would never sully himself by touching lips that had touched Mickey Rourke's.

What a blow, then, when I turned on the television one awful evening to hear Mary Hart chirpily announcing that not only was Alec really dating that horrible bitch but he was going to marry her. My man — my Alec — was actually going to give himself to the woman who not only couldn't act to save her life but who had gone out and bought a whole town. Even on my worst shopping days, I had never returned home with more than a pair of shoes. And I sincerely doubted that Kim even knew what a little linen guest towel was.

I didn't understand it. How could Alec — my Alec — the man who spoke so eloquently about politics, acting, and human rights — the man who won accolades for his serious stage work, be marrying the human equivalent of cotton candy? It was yet another senseless act in a world gone awry. I went into a tailspin.

Lest you think that my love for Alec is based solely on his on-screen image, I should tell you that I have met Alec in person twice in my life. Okay, I've seen Alec in person twice in my life. The first time was when he played Stanley in the revival of Tennessee Williams's *A Streetcar Named Desire* on Broadway. I was first in line the day the box office opened. When the woman behind the ticket window asked me what kind of seats I wanted, I answered breathlessly, "As close to Alec as I can get" and flung my Gold Card at her.

Now, normally I wouldn't bother to plunk down $75 to watch some guy in a play. But the real genius of Tennessee Williams is that he was, when it came down to it, a frustrated queen, and consequently most of his leading men spend a great deal of time running about in undershirts and boxers. Because the parts are so gripping, the male stars seldom realize that the entire point of a Williams play is to see hunky men seminude. This makes it all a great deal of fun for the rest of us, who are in on the joke and wish that more actors would venture into live theater.

I do not actually remember much about the play. I'm sure Jessica Lange, who was also in it, was brilliant. After all, she won raves for it, even though I suspect the critics applauded her simply because she was able to touch Alec's chest while still retaining the ability to speak complete sentences. And I'm told that the writing is very good for that sort of thing. All I can vividly recall is that Alec took his shirt off six times during the two and a half hours he was onstage. In fact, the entire production seemed to have been conveniently choreographed around opportunities for Alec to undress. Whoever staged the thing should have won a Tony for it.

Alec himself was nominated for a Tony, and I have no doubt that this had less to do with the forcefulness with which he screamed out "Hey, Stella!" than it did with his nightly striptease. I am not exaggerating in the least when I tell you that every time Alec reached for the buttons on his shirt, the entire house fell completely silent. When he casually shucked off the shirt and peeled his sweat-soaked T-shirt over his head to reveal his beautiful hairy chest, there was an audible gasp from every sensible person in the audience, the vast majority of whom were male. It was a moment I will never forget. Had my American Express card allowed it, I would have bought box seats for the entire run.

This brings us back to the night I discovered Alec was getting married. Tragically, the second time I saw Alec was on the day before his wedding to She Who Is Unworthy to Run Her Tongue Over His Chest. After hearing the news of the impending nuptials, I had called in sick for a week, unable to get out of bed except to change the Alec tape in my VCR. Finally, after wearing out my copy of *The Hunt for Red October*, I'd pulled myself together and returned to work. It was my first day back, I had somehow muddled through despite my pain, and I was coming home from my office in Midtown. I'd managed to get a cab at Second Avenue and 52nd Street. It was raining, as well as a Friday afternoon, and this was no small accomplishment. For a brief moment, I thought maybe things were looking up.

As the cab rushed past the corner of 48th Street, I noticed a man waving for a taxi. In the true manner of a New Yorker possessed of a cab while others wait in the rain, I laughed wickedly to myself. Until we got closer, and I realized that it was Alec — my Alec — standing there, rain running down his manly face and onto his coat as he vainly tried to flag a ride. Suddenly, everything seemed to move in slow motion. It was just like a scene from a 1940s love story. I pressed my face against the glass and wailed his name as we raced by. Try as I might, the Pakistani driver would not stop the cab, even when I grabbed him by the hair and screamed, "You don't understand — I must get my hands on that chest!" We sped down Second Avenue as I cursed the fact that real life seldom turns out like a Billy Wilder film.

Little did I know that Alec was, in fact, at that very moment on his way to his wedding in Long Island. When I saw it on the news later that evening, with a triumphant Kim smiling as she dragged an obviously confused Alec down the aisle, I wept bitterly. Fate had thrown me

57

another chance, and I'd blown it. When I'd left him on that corner, I'd ruined forever any chance we might have had. I knew it was all over for me and Alec. I did the only thing a jilted lover can do. I bought sixteen bags of Reese's Peanut Butter Cups, put my worn-out copy of *Beetlejuice* in the VCR, and ate myself into a stupor.

In the days after, I tried to cope as best I could. At first, I hoped the marriage would fall apart in the tradition of so many other ill-suited Hollywood couplings. Surely Alec would quickly see what a mistake he'd made and divest himself of the walking Barbie he'd given himself to. Then I would rush in to comfort the man who obviously had been destined for me all along, laughing cruelly at Kim as I put Alec's bags in my trunk and drove away to a secluded cabin in Vermont. Smiling sweetly, I would roll down my window and reduce her to tears with the two cruelest words I could think of: "*Boxing Helena.*"

But he didn't leave her. In fact, over the next year or so, Alec and Kim seemed to become one of those rarities in Hollywood — a bizarre couple who manage to remain together despite the fact that they have absolutely nothing in common. Just like Bruce and Demi, they inexplicably weathered everything from financial ruin to critical potshots at their films without a scratch. Not only did they thrive in the face of adversity but they did it shamelessly.

Kim Basinger, of course, became my enemy. I rented her movies, searching them for some sign of the elusive quality possessed by the shameless hussy who had stolen my husband right out from under me. Like Venus Williams watching tapes of Martina Hingis to prepare a game plan, I studied her every move. She had to have something I didn't have, something that drove Alec crazy, and I was determined to find it and duplicate it. I watched *9½ Weeks, Batman,* and *Cool World* until I was sure my eyes would begin to bleed. I analyzed the way Kim flipped her hair, dissected her amazing ability to speak without ever moving her lips, and strived to copy her capacity to render a full range of emotions meaningless with the same vacant stare.

My friends begged me to stop my madness. "Please," my friend Katherine said. "Switch to Billy. At least he isn't married." This, of course, was pre–Chynna Phillips. But I wouldn't hear of it. "His face is too bony," I said, kissing my picture of Alec with a full day's growth of beard. "Try Danny," said another well-meaning soul, and I was briefly tempted, until I heard him talk. "Too stupid," I said decidedly, replaying my tape of Alec fervently discussing environmental issues on *Crossfire* with John Sununu and imagining myself walking a picket line with him, his manly hand gripped in mine. I suspected Kim's idea of saving the environment was using biodegradable bleach.

In the end, of course, my battle proved fruitless. Despite numerous voodoo dolls, rituals, prayers, and candle burnings, as of this writing Alec remains with Kim. They've even managed to produce a child, dashing my long-held hope that perhaps the relationship was never consummated and that Alec was holding out for me, wondering why I was so late in coming. When he decked the photographer trying to snap a photo of him on the way home from the hospital, I knew in my heart that it was out of frustration at not having found me.

Unable to have him for my own, I have devoted my life to celibacy. If I can't have Alec, I want no one. No other mouth will kiss mine. No other hands will caress my flesh. I have resigned myself to an existence devoid of love. Oh, sure, I've tried dating, but inevitably it ends up the same way every time. No matter how witty, charming, and handsome the man, at the end of the evening when he asks for another date, I sigh, look into his eyes, and say sadly, "I'm sorry, but you're just no Alec." Like an unlucky princess in one of the sadder Grimm's tales, I am cursed to wander the world alone while another enjoys my beloved's bed.

Still, there may be signs of hope for me yet. A few weeks ago, I read in a gossip column that Alec had started going to a salon to have his back hair removed, after Kim said it repulsed her and refused to do it for him anymore. All I have to say is, Kim, you better watch out, you bitch. Because I, for one, will be waiting outside the door with hot wax in hand.

The Sound of Music

During the decade in which I lived in New York, I saw three Broadway shows. One was *Lettice and Lovage*, a play that starred Maggie Smith and Margaret Tyzack and was very, very funny. The second was *A Streetcar Named Desire*, which starred Alec Baldwin's chest and was very, very refreshing. The third was *Gypsy*, which starred Tyne Daley and was neither of the above.

You see, I dare to stand in defiance of one of the most cherished of gay male traditions: I do not like musical shows. In fact, I will stretch my neck out even further and announce once and for right-here-in-public all that I dislike Barbra Streisand as well. There, I've said it. Start throwing stones.

Now, everyone knows that the only reason homosexuals live in New York is so they can attend Broadway shows. Therefore, being someone who doesn't even know who Patti LuPone is proved to be a decided disadvantage in my life there. While my friends rushed off for evenings of *Sunset Boulevard* and *Phantom,* I mumbled excuses and bolted for home and safety. When out-of-town acquaintances would phone, asking advice on what to see when they came to The City for the weekend, I feverishly pawed through the Sunday *Times,* hoping the ads would provide some clues and I wouldn't be revealed as the theater dunce that I am.

This aversion to musical theater began early in my life, when my mother decided it would be fun for the family to trek out to a production of *The Music Man* starring the odder half of *The Odd Couple*, Tony Randall. I sat, horrified, as grown men and women twirled and bounced across the stage in costumes straight out of *Mary Poppins*. Even worse, they all sang, including Tony. They sang while walking. They sang while dancing. They just kept singing. I knew this didn't happen in real life, and it confused me. Why, I wondered, didn't our mailman belt out a jaunty chorus as he popped letters into the box? How come my father, spurred to heights of joy by the appearance of a parade, never produced a cane and hat and did a little dance? A decidedly cynical child, I immediately suspected that someone was having a joke at my expense, and I didn't appreciate it.

A few months later, my mother announced that we were going on a trip to Vermont. Completely unsuspecting, I eagerly hopped in the car and went. When we arrived at a quaint mountain inn, I was indeed surprised. Then we went inside.

"Do you remember that movie we saw about the children in Austria?" my mother asked as she registered at the desk. "You remember, *The Sound of Music?*"

I nodded, confused. I did remember the movie. I had even enjoyed it to some degree, mainly because the children in it were horrid and had gotten, albeit accidentally, to swim in a river, something I was forbidden to do at any costs. I had no idea what it had to do with the inn or Vermont or me.

"Well," my mother said, "have I got a surprise for you. When that family escaped from Austria, they came here and started this inn. We're going to meet them."

For a moment I was completely thrilled. Although I had little use for musicals, I was easily overwhelmed by the thought of celebrities. Once my father had wrangled us seats in the presidential box at the Kennedy Center, and I had taken great delight in peeing in the same toilet Jimmy Carter used. The thought of meeting actual movie stars made my head swim.

I was beside myself until dinner, when the Von Trapps were to make their appearance in the sitting room. At the appointed hour, the guests gathered in the room and waited. A door opened, and in walked several elderly people dressed in costumes. None of them was wearing shorts made out of draperies.

"Who are they?" I asked my mother, pointing at the aged women and men seating themselves in chairs.

"Those are the children," she said.

"Where are their costumes?"

"That was just a movie," she said. "These are the real people. Now look, here comes Maria."

I turned and looked, expecting a young woman to frisk into the room with a guitar. Instead, what came in was the oldest woman I'd ever seen, led by two slightly younger but equally wrinkled women. They took her to a chair, where she sat down heavily and smiled wanly, as though being trotted out as an exhibit was hardly the most exhilarating thing she had to do that day. "Welcome," she said in a whisper, as though speaking any more loudly would cause her to crumble into dust.

One by one, the guests went up and shook hands with the eldest Von Trapp. Some of them wept openly.

All of them hugged her. When it was our turn, my mother took my hand and dragged me up to the chair. Eyeing Maria dubiously, I stood and scuffed the floor with my shoe.

"This is Michael," my mother said. "He loved the movie about you."

"Did you?" she asked.

I stared at her for a long moment. "Why aren't you dead yet?" I asked finally, unable to think of anything else.

The trip home was a grim one. Years later, my first editor would tell me that in elementary school she had as her teacher one of the youngest Von Trapp daughters, who had become a nun like her stepmother. Seeing the cheerful *Sound of Music* children on television and then facing the ruler-carrying real-life Von Trapp specimen in class had so unnerved this woman that she couldn't hear even a single song from the movie without going into hysterics. I know how she feels.

Things got worse as I grew older and realized that I was surrounded by people who not only liked musicals but who thought it was fun to participate in them. My sisters listened endlessly to *Jesus Christ Superstar.* Annual viewings of *West Side Story* were encouraged. In high school, which unfortunately for me coincided with the popularity of films like *Fame* and *Flashdance,* one enterprising teacher informed us that we would be putting on a show he'd written based on the wretched Styx album *Paradise Theater.* I was told I would have to sing, solo, some absurd song, which after hearing the words of I was convinced had to do with a man taking his mother to Africa and not enjoying it very much. Perhaps I was wrong, but we'll never know. I conveniently broke my arm and got out of it. I still insist I fell out of the tree by accident.

College was better, as I attended a highly religious school where, among numerous other things, we were forbidden to attend Broadway musicals because the content was considered less than seemly. Since the school was only half an hour from New York by train, this was a very real concern to the God-fearing folks who supervised our education, and the moratorium on musical theater was one of the only edicts set down by the school's governing body that I accepted as plain good sense, even if I didn't wholly agree with the reason.

Imagine my horror, then, when after graduation I went to live in Greenwich Village and discovered that not only was the singing of show tunes considered acceptable by reasonable people but it was practically mandatory. Just as in *The Music Man,* I could barely walk down my block without someone breaking into song and tossing flowers into the air. On my first visit ever to a gay bar, I entered warily, only to be surrounded by a chorus of manly voices belting out the words to "Over the Rainbow." I stood, staring at the crowd around the piano, and wept.

I tried to fit in. I really did. I spent evenings at bars like Eighty-Eights and Don't Tell Mama. I bought the original cast albums (which I very quickly learned never to call sound tracks) to popular shows and played them. But it was no use. I just didn't like it. While others laughed lightly and called out their favorite songs to the piano player, I sipped my beer and wished I was home watching TV. I didn't get the sly references to *Guys and Dolls* and *Showboat.* I felt like Herbie, that elf in *Rudolph the Red-nosed Reindeer,* the one who wants to be a dentist instead of making toys. Eventually, of course, I had to move out of the city in shame.

I don't like musicals for the same reason I don't like opera: I do not believe that sane people should express their feelings in loud tones of voice. If you are sad, I do not want to hear about it in sweeping movements accompanied by a thirty-piece orchestra. If you have just fallen in love with the most wonderful boy or girl in the world, chances are you're the only one who thinks it's really swell, and leaping onto a bench and crowing about it will not make you any friends. Do you have a problem so intense you feel you must share it with the world? Trust me, singing about it won't help. Shut up.

Now, I'm not totally against musicals. I do recall with some fondness purchasing the sound tracks to *Grease* and *Saturday Night Fever* and singing along in the rec room. And somewhere in my record collection is a copy of *Xanadu*. But that's the extent of it. And I was ten. I also thought Farrah Fawcett was really cool, and I wore a green satin baseball jacket because Shaun Cassidy did. I have since moved on. Unfortunately, some of my contemporaries seem not to have and are now bombarding the world with things like *Rent* and revivals of *Hair.* They should be ashamed of themselves.

Part of the problem is that this is not the '70s, when things like musical theater seemed perfectly natural and, in comparison to Vicki Sue Robinson and *Welcome Back, Kotter,* positively brilliant. Everyone was singing then, so why not put it on stage, dress it up in fun costumes, and sell tickets? But we know better now. Sure, we think going to the Kiss reunion tour is fun, and it is. But do we really need to drag *Grease* back out of the trunk, put Brooke Shields in it, and pretend it was the greatest moment of our lives? At least Gene Simmons knows he looks silly in his platform dragon boots, and we love him all the more for spitting blood at us while we rock and roll all night just one more time.

I think perhaps I would like musical theater if it didn't take itself so seriously. For example, what if instead of Maureen McCormick and John Stamos as Sandy and Danny in the *Grease* revival we had, say, the Dalai Lama and Camille Paglia? "You're the one that I want," the Dalai would croon as he boogied in the Shake Shack. "Tell me about it, stud," Camille would say, pitching her cigarette to the ground and throwing her shoulders back. The audience, shocked out of its stupor, would go wild. Or what if instead of Julie Andrews romping around on stage hamming it up in *Victor/Victoria* we had, oh, Al Gore accompanied by some gaily dressed members of the Senate as a chorus. Now that would be fun. And I bet he'd show up at the Tony's ready to perform.

But no, what we have instead is *Cats*. Okay, I admit the idea of a bunch of singing cats was entertaining when I was six. But at twenty-nine, I find it merely irritating. And I have seen *Cats*, although I have spent many years in therapy trying to forget the event. All I recall now is that the entire row ahead of me was filled with a group of high school students from Ohio. They all wore the same outfits they'd worn to their prom, and they thought they were very sophisticated. The theater crackled as satin-covered behinds settled into the seats, and the air was heavy with the smell of Aqua Net and Obsession for Men. The enthusiastic theatergoers clapped after every "meow" and swish of a tail. When the time came for Betty Buckley to sing "Memory," one of the boys fainted.

See, that's the problem with musicals. They pretend to be real art enhanced by some catchy songs, but all they really are underneath the costumes and sets are the Enchanted Tiki Room and Country Bear Jamboree from Walt Disney World shoved into a building with a grand name, peevish ushers, and no legroom. But because the ticket costs $85, people who should know better think it's something to get excited about.

In fact, if you look closely, you will see that underneath the pretty costumes and lavish sets, all musicals are really Disney movies. Think about it — every successful animated Disney film has relied heavily on catchy tunes to sweep the action along. Where would *Snow White* be without "Some Day My Prince Will Come" or *Lady and the Tramp* without "The Siamese Cat Song"? Sure, musicals were around long before Disney, but isn't it suspicious that more and more, Broadway shows look like cartoons come to life? Is it so difficult to imagine Andrew Lloyd Weber's phantom singing "Whistle While You Work" or *Les Mis*'s Cosette warbling "When You Wish Upon a Star"?

This is Broadway's secret shame. Writers and producers will do anything to convince us that their shows aren't just expensive versions of movies we could rent for $3 and enjoy in the comfort of our own homes, but mostly they're just variations on *Pinocchio* and *Bambi*. The truth of this is evidenced by the fact that when Disney announced plans to open a theater in New York and put on a production of *Beauty and the Beast*, the Broadway elite proclaimed the show nothing more than candy for the masses of unwashed tourists (much as the filmmaking community cried foul when the movie version was nominated for an Oscar and did better box office than the other four nominees combined). Undaunted, Disney went ahead. The show went on to be the season's biggest and only hit, undoubtedly due to millions of people from Ohio wearing prom dresses and plastic shoes. But fans of musical theater refused to accept this young upstart into their arms, insisting that their own shows were, well, just better.

I'm curious to know where the Broadway glitterati draw the line. Is Tony darling Nathan Lane darting about in a toga that reveals far more than anyone wants to see really any more dignified or deserving of praise than a giant singing candlestick dancing with a talking clock? Given a choice of the two, I'd be hard-pressed to choose, although I give the edge to the candlestick and the clock simply because I haven't quite forgiven Lane for singing "Hakuna Matata" in *The Lion King*.

And hey, now that I think of it, wasn't that a Disney movie too? Perhaps that line between Hollywood and Broadway is blurring a little bit more. Or maybe the folks on the Great White Way are finally accepting the inevitable — if they want to keep working, they have to get their noses out of the air and take a look at what America really likes to watch. It seems that in the battle between high art and popular culture, the little mouse with the funny pants and the squeaky voice is still kicking everyone's ass.

Why I Hate Shopping

I do not like to shop. At all. For anything.

I used to think this was because as a child I spent a great deal of my life being dragged around by my mother while she searched for the perfect pair of navy blue pumps. Any shopping trip inevitably turned into a quest for The Pumps, with my mother scanning store after store for the elusive footwear while I wailed pleas for mercy. "Aren't those the right color?" I'd sob as she picked up the three thousandth pair of perfectly adequate-looking blue shoes we'd seen that afternoon and examined them closely. I'd hold my breath and wait, collapsing into hysterics when she shook her head and said brightly, "Just this one more store."

Many years and much therapy later, my mother still does not have her navy blue pumps and I understand this is not the reason I hate shopping. I hate it because being in the proximity of so many things to buy makes me hyperventilate not because I want them but because the idea of so many lives spent making all the things and then even more lives spent convincing people they need the things and then even more lives spent selling the things and working to be able to buy the things makes me twitch with rage. Every time I see something truly awful — for example, a T-shirt emblazoned with kittens drawn in glitter — I am struck by the realization that not only did someone have to sit down and consciously decide to create that T-shirt, but then someone else had to spend at least part of her or his life manufacturing it, someone else designed a marketing strategy for it, someone else ordered it, and now someone else was actively selling it to someone who would actually buy and wear it. The fact that the sum total of probably one whole life was spent making that stupid glittery kitten T-shirt makes me want to cry. That's why I do not go shopping.

On the rare occasions when I *do* go shopping, inevitably I am overcome by the horror of being surrounded by so many useless things. And the frightening part is — I am fairly easily convinced that I need to purchase them. Obviously I have to own another pair of sandals; the current ones are running down a bit. A new linen shirt from J. Crew? But of course — you never know when you'll be invited to that clambake on the Vineyard. Before I know it, I've become a maelstrom of buying, flinging my Visa card at unsuspecting sales clerks as I dash from store to store until, breathless, I stagger out loaded down with parcels and bags, boxes and receipts. Then I look down at my perfectly good sandals and weep.

It's happened again. The last time I tried to go to shopping, I needed only to pick up Q-Tips. (The dog had an ear infection.) Three days later, I returned with seventeen pairs of socks, a baseball glove, three candles shaped like winged horses, a white-noise machine, four kinds of freshly baked cookies, a goose-down duvet, and all of Olivia Newton-John's albums on CD. The only thing I didn't have was the Q-Tips.

For many years I lived in New York, where shopping is not a problem, primarily because everything is far too expensive to actually buy. And since stores in New York invariably specialize in just one thing, shopping is easy. Limited as you are to purchasing the single item you need, there is no temptation to "just pick up" additional things or to browse through aisle after aisle of other things you hadn't thought to buy but are suddenly overcome with a need to purchase. If you need new shoes, you go to the shoe store. A nice ham, the ham store. Intriguing new sex toys, the sex-toy store. In New York, consumerism, like everything else, is very regimented. There are, of course, enormous department stores like Macy's and Lord & Taylor's, but they are to be avoided at all costs because they are crawling with thin young people dressed entirely in black who spritz you with various perfumes while chanting, "Obsession for Men," which is not, as it might at first seem, a question. The experience, I imagine, is probably not unlike attending a Hitler Youth meeting where everyone smelled nice and worked on commission.

But I no longer live in New York. And in the rest of America, shopping is a far deadlier undertaking. You can imagine my horror, then, when one day I went to change the sheets and realized that there was simply not a pair left with the elastic intact and without various unidentifiable stains mottling them like some kind of weird body fluid-food-pet stain batik. It just wouldn't do. I had to buy new ones, and that meant going shopping.

I decided to go to Filene's, primarily because it was the only store I could actually remember ever seeing in Boston, and it was close by on the subway. I could get off, get my sheets, and be home within an hour. While it wouldn't be enjoyable, it would at least be painless.

Or so I thought.

Getting there was fine. I got on the T when it came and got off again eight stops later at Downtown Crossing. I exited the turnstile and proceeded immediately to the entrance to Filene's. This was when I realized my first crucial mistake. Upon exiting the T station, I found the street swarming with people. It was lunch hour, which meant that approximately 8 billion people were scurrying about downtown Boston trying to complete their errands before grabbing something to eat and returning to work.

Taking a deep breath, I darted across Winter Street, weaving between men in dark suits and women with smart dresses. Arriving on the other side relatively unharmed, I congratulated myself and headed for the door to Filene's.

That was when I stumbled upon my second crucial mistake. You see, I'd forgotten that, like Macy's, Filene's is really just an entire mall crammed into one store. This means that everything detestable about a mall is amplified about 10,000 times by the mere fact of being contained in a smaller space. Once I got through the door, I was met not with the sounds of Prozac-like music of the 1980s but by the feverish screams of a frenzied mob of Hispanic housewives. They were all running about excitedly waving their arms in the air, as though someone had just caught a glimpse of the Virgin Mary in a Wonderbra and everyone was dying to see it before it degenerated into just another 32A cup.

I flattened myself against the wall as a large woman charged past, her arms filled with half slips and her eyes rolled back in her head. "What the hell is going on?" I said.

73

"It's a sale!" someone screamed as she sailed past me on her way to a table overflowing with black knee socks. Before I could thank her for the information, she went down like a wounded deer, felled by a woman holding up the last pair of socks in triumph.

Apparently I had wandered smack into the middle of some kind of radio promotion being put on by a Latin music station. A deejay had taken over the center of the floor and was chattering ceaselessly as the shopping women swarmed around him. "Who'd like another ten percent off?" he crowed in his faux-masculine deejay voice.

"We do!" screamed the women as one, the spittle flying from their lips as they ran panting from rack to rack.

I spied the escalator across the room. There was no way I was going to reach it what with all the women creating crosscurrents everywhere I turned. Like sharks worked up into a feeding frenzy, they were out of control, grabbing and pushing in the quest for bargains. I needed to create a diversion.

"Hey!" I shouted. "Isn't that a size sixteen Lanz nightgown over there?" I called out recklessly.

The flow turned instantly, with every woman in the store charging for the sleepwear. As the aisle near me cleared, I took advantage of it and sped across the floor. As I ascended into the upper reaches of Filene's, the din of voices became a dull roar.

Upstairs, things were calmer. I leisurely made my way to linens and started to search for sheets. I wanted plain white cotton sheets. Nothing fancy. What I saw were rows and rows of gaily colored sheets in vibrant colors. There were displays of cheerful sheets created by designers such as Ralph Lauren and Laura Ashley. Their bright flowers and sporty plaids called out, and I felt the familiar spell falling over me. Maybe I did need some nice green-checked Polo sheets.

I picked up a package. $129.95 for a sheet. Just one. And I needed at least two, plus pillowcases. The spell lifted. But they were very attractive, as was the man in the photo on the package. Maybe if I had sheets like this, I could have a man like this as well. Maybe he came as part of the set. I quickly moved away. Somehow, the spell became weaker the farther away I got. I wondered briefly if there was some chemical included in Ralph Lauren sheets that made them irresistible to gay men. Pheromones, maybe. That could explain Calvin Klein underwear as well.

I searched the entire section, to no avail. I found purple sheets, sheets with birds, abstract sheets, even black sheets. But no actual white sheets. I did find a lot of sheets that looked white to me, but they all had names like china, bone, and, still inexplicable to me, Marilyn. The closest thing they had to plain old white was a set of creamy linen sheets with satin ribbon edging. They were called angelwhite, and they cost $85. Maybe for Martha Stewart's country home, but not for me.

Finally, a clerk appeared from the recesses of the store like a prophet sent to deliver the wisdom of Jehovah to the ignorant. His hair was neatly greased back, and he looked like he knew a lot about bedding. His name was Geoff.

"Can I help you?" he asked politely.

"I need sheets," I said confidently. "White sheets."

"White?" Geoff said, as though he'd never heard of the color before.

"Yes," I said. "White."

"How about eggshell?" he suggested, starting for the Laura Ashley section.

"No," I said quickly. "Just white. Plain white."

"What about this lovely buttermilk Vera Wang bed ensemble?" he tried, waving a $625 set at me.

I could see where this was heading. "No buttermilk," I said. "And no ensemble. I just want sheets. White sheets. No eggshell. No winter. No ennui. Definitely no Marilyn. No whatever they call it. Just white."

Geoff's demeanor changed. "Fine," he said shortly. He led me to a dark corner of the store. "Normally we don't put these out," he said, "but we had some left."

He pointed at a stack of sheets carelessly tossed in a jumble on the floor. They looked a lot like the Laura Ashley, Ralph Lauren, and Vera Wang eggshell-buttermilk-Marilyn-winter sheets. But they said WHITE on them in little letters, like it was a guilty sin to be so ordinary.

"Most of our customers prefer the more unique shades," Geoff said, as though I'd just asked for Cheese Whiz and Wonder bread.

"Most of your customers are downstairs wrestling over a bra," I informed him. I picked up a set of sheets (only $39.95), paid, and left. As I exited the store, I rejoiced in what was, for me, a successful shopping trip, made even happier by the fact that I wouldn't have to repeat the endeavor for another five years or so. I hopped onto the T and breathed a sigh of relief.

Back at home, I pulled my hard-won sheets from the bag and looked gleefully at the package.

They were the wrong size.

The Perils of Dating

I am not good at dating.

Mind you, this isn't just some sudden gloomy thought brought on by an annoying dry spell between thrilling romantic encounters. This is based on the indisputable fact that over the last seven years I have had approximately three dates, none of which I can actually recall and none of which was repeated.

I suppose it's my fault, really. I never know how it's all supposed to work. My parents, from all accounts virgins on their wedding night, had exactly one date, which consisted of attending a church picnic surrounded by beaming elders. One of my sisters married at nineteen after dating only two men, and the other ran off with an unsavory character just to prove some point that, much to her enduring annoyance, none of us every fully got. Even my forebears are no help — one grandmother became pregnant, and I swear I am not making this up, while living in a convent; the other had four husbands, leaving me forever in doubt as to my mother's maiden name when asked for it by surly bank managers. With such meager experience to draw on, it's a wonder I haven't ended up padding around a trailer in a muumuu while my ex-con boyfriend bellows for another Hostess Snowball and a can of Genesee Creme

Ale so he can thoroughly enjoy the breathtaking thrill of *Cops*.

Let us also not forget that I am of the generation reared on the magic of Disney. Countless viewings of *Cinderella* and *Sleeping Beauty* as a child left me with the firm impression that all I'd have to do to attain romantic fulfillment was lounge around pining and eventually some handsome man with perfect teeth would happen by and be struck by my lonely beauty. We would then repair to some fabulous castle, accompanied by the chirps and trills of cartoon birds, and spend the rest of our lives being deliriously happy in a generally cheerful, if not sexually explicit, kind of way.

Imagine my horror, then, when I found out the whole affair actually involved the wanton exchanging of phone numbers and trying to fall asleep with my hero's slumbering head making my arm numb. I have a difficult time accepting that Snow White was forced to endure Prince Charming's suggestions that water sports might be interesting, and picturing her going through his drawers while he was out hunting to see what other princesses he'd been slipping it to ruins the whole dream utterly. If you ask me, being a cartoon heroine isn't all it's cracked up to be when the curtain comes down and the prince goes back to hunting Bambi's mother with the guys.

Walt's lies aside, I am willing to accept some of the blame for this problem of not yet being partnered. My friend Grace says it's because I'm not serious enough. Maybe she's right. With the exception of supermodels and Playboy bunnies, who inevitably list humor as the most desirable quality in the man of their dreams, most people seem to rank it far beneath being steadily employed and having perfect abs. The thought that

Naomi Campbell would find me utterly enthralling has its appeal, but on the whole I'd rather have George Clooney banging on my bedroom door.

Nor does it help that I'm completely oblivious when someone is interested. I do not know when I am being cruised. I think men who smile at me knowingly are looking at something amusing behind me. I once had a man I was intensely fascinated with kiss me for a full three minutes on a crowded New York street in front of a whole phalanx of firefighters battling a restaurant grease-fire inferno. Afterward, I politely said good night, went home alone, and wondered for days if he liked me. It never occurred to me that sticking his tongue down my throat before an audience of toasting diners might be a clue. I thought he was just being nice. By the time I figured it out, months later, he'd moved on to someone with more highly developed dating skills.

Curious to see if I was the only one with this deficiency, I called my friend Sybil, also single. "Are you dating anyone?" I asked innocently, hoping she'd say she wasn't and we could then bitch about it for an hour or so.

"No one special," she answered. "A couple of different people."

A couple of different people! She said it so casually. The thought astounded me. How can anyone date a couple of different people. Maybe it's just me, but the minute I start dating someone, or even get introduced in passing, I instantly become a neurotic mess. Okay, I was probably neurotic long before the dating even started, but the first date inevitably sets off a predictable pattern. No matter that we've shared only one night of Thai food — I must know where it's all leading. If he doesn't call, he must hate me, or he's sleeping with someone else. If he does call, I wonder why he doesn't have anyone else to hang out with. You can see the dilemma. I would hardly have the time to stalk more than one person at a time.

The casual dating thing may be what the carefree queers of the '90s are into, but it just doesn't do it for me. I don't like being around strangers enough to date someone if I don't think that joint checking and rooms filled with IKEA furnishings aren't a definite possibility. I don't need to sit through boring movies or endless hockey games just so we can get to know each other and feel that we have fulfilling interpersonal relationships. I am quite secure in my dysfunction and do not need to pretend that my life has meaning outside of watching Bruce Willis movies. I have an entire owner's manual already typed up. I simply hand it over on the first date and tell him to call with any questions.

This whole notion of casual sex also leaves me cold. In the time it would take me to find someone, discuss who would do what to whom, and do it, I could have eaten an entire Entenmann's pound cake and spent several amusing hours replaying the scene in *The Color of Night* where Bruce Willis pulls off his boxers and gives an all-too-brief shot of his ass and willy. As for the sex part, I could accomplish the same thing by myself, and without having to take a shower, leave the house, or wonder why there were two toothbrushes in his bathroom and a second pair of glasses on the bedside table.

No, I am looking for more. In pursuit of this dream, I trotted dolefully to the local gay bookstore and picked up a copy of a self-help book whose blurbs promised that reading it would ensure romantic success. I will not embarrass the author by revealing his name, because he is a frightful liar. To be sure, the book was filled with all manner of sage advice about seeking out the mate of one's dreams. I learned that I must first love myself if anyone was to love me and that I have no one to blame but myself for consistently passing over well-adjusted, happy men for those with criminal records and enormous endowments. But this I already knew.

Where the book really failed was in its suggestions for actually finding a man once I'd cleared away all of the emotional debris I'd built up over the years. I should, the author suggested helpfully, think of men as squirrels. And squirrels, naturally, are searching for nuts. In particular, squirrels want large, attractive, meaty nuts. *Don't we all,* I thought as I turned the page, curious to see where this whole squirrel thing was going. It was there that I learned that I am, in fact, the nut, which was not as disconcerting as it probably should have been. Furthermore, if I wanted to attract a squirrel with a particularly bushy tail and a cheerful outlook on life, the book said, I must be an especially wonderful nut. Because the best squirrels always have the best nuts. *Maybe I should just date squirrels,* I thought joylessly as I tossed the book aside.

The problem, ultimately, is that dating involves men, and men are hard to find these days. Oh, sure, there are scads of annoying fellows doused in Obsession for Men just lying about for the taking. But the really good ones, the ones who like big dogs and don't care what Madonna is up to today, are fair near extinct. When I do find one that might be interesting, his wife always comes along to spoil it.

It also does not help that I am the least social human being on this planet, making the normal avenues of meeting people closed to me. I do not go to parties. I do not attend readings and literary functions, usually wonderful places for writer types to meet men, at least men who can read. Unfortunately, these types of men have never appealed to me, as they are frequently disposed to having ideas about things, which they want to discuss at length. This is intolerable. Bars are also not an option, if only because I do not see well in dim light and become easily confused by the noise and smoke common to such places, which within minutes renders me into something of a cross between a hysterical beaver trying to remove itself from a leg trap and a political prisoner being forced to stare at a naked bulb while unpleasant people with loud voices ask questions to which I do not know the answers.

I've tried the volunteer route as well, spending several months working at a community center hoping that, while doing some good, I might also encounter some nice ex-jock with a house in the country and the courtesy to think that everything I do is amazing. Sadly, while I did learn lots of clever cheers to toss around at rallies of all kinds, in the end I found it difficult to relate to men whose primary concern was for which nipple to get pierced. And forget meeting men through friends. My friends do not know anyone I would ever want to go out with. In fact, I don't even want to go anywhere with them, so why would I trust their judgment.

When I do, by chance, meet someone who might even possibly be date material, I have developed a remarkable system for going through an entire relationship with the person in my mind in thirty seconds flat. I whiz through dating and the first sexual encounter to moving in together and buying a dog in no time. By the time I've even walked across the room, I already have us fighting over the VCR as he packs his things to leave, making introductions irrelevant because we are no longer speaking. It saves a lot of time.

It's not that I'm particularly fussy. In fact, I don't ask for much. But what I do ask for is hard to find these days — a man who is independent, believes in himself, and questions the state of the world. Unfortunately, these men are almost always either married to Kim Basinger or they're career criminals. As my friend Dan cruelly pointed out recently: "Your problem is that your ideal man is the Unabomber." Sad, but true.

Still, ever the romantic, I refuse to stop believing that somewhere out there is a man I can, if not love madly, at least tolerate. So here's the plan: I am having an essay contest, and the grand prize is me. Anyone interested is free to submit. All you have to do is tell me in 750 words or less how you are going to make me wildly excited forever. Essays will be judged on originality, penmanship, and ability to amuse me. Presents are also a nice touch, especially cash. The winner will be notified by my arrival on his doorstep.

Okay, so it isn't Ed McMahon handing you a big check with lots of zeros. But at least you don't have to lick seventy-three different stamps and put them in the right places to win.

Picture Imperfect

I do not like to have my picture taken.

This is not a mere paranoia; it is an out-and-out mania. I do not pose for group shots during outings with friends. I do not think spontaneous camera clicking is cheery and whimsical. I firmly believe that people who were the photo editors of their high school yearbooks all grew up to work for the Department of Motor Vehicles and wear unpleasant fabric blends.

The analytically inclined among my friends say this aversion to being photographed is because I have issues with how I look. That's not true. I'm perfectly happy with the way I look. I simply have issues with being locked in a frame and stared at by people I only marginally like.

When I was a child, this wasn't the problem it might at first appear to be. For one thing, I was a third child, with ten years coming between me and my two older sisters, whom my mother had enthusiastically conceived less than a year apart. Despite my being of a different gender, and thus a novelty, my parents apparently decided that all babies do, in fact, look like Winston Churchill, and chose not to add any further pictures to albums already crammed with close-ups of infants with interchangeable expressions.

Thankfully, neither of my parents was particularly interested in capturing our lives on film anyway. While there were reams of photos taken of the first few birthdays and holidays of my sisters' lives, this ended abruptly somewhere around the time of my eldest sister's sixth birthday, as though having finally figured out how to keep the camera in focus, my father had decided that the game was no longer amusing. After that, all there is to mark our growth are a few shots taken at random moments, generally by people other than our parents. The sole picture of me from those dreamy years of childhood shows me shaking hands with Ranger Rick, the raccoon mascot of the nature magazine of the same name. It was taken by an overenthusiastic friend of my mother's, whose child was also along for the historic event. Despite my joy at meeting this hero of my youth, my face sports a decidedly bitter look.

Besides, even if they had been inclined toward picture-taking, neither my father nor my mother could ever accurately recall what was depicted in any given photo anyway. Never ones for writing the dates or occasions on the backs of snapshots, a typical look through a stack of pictures went something like this.

"Oh, look, that's our house in Hawaii," my mother would say, peering at the blurry shot of something resembling palm trees and water.

"No, it's not," my father would counter. "It's from our trip to Kenya."

"But that's your mother there, standing by the palm tree."

"I think that's a native totem, actually."

Inevitably, after half an hour of trying to distinguish old houses from long-deceased pets and children from national monuments, they would give up in disgust, tossing all of the photos back into the box and storing it once more on the top shelf of the linen closet, where it would languish until the next time someone worked up the courage to do it all again.

It was a simple matter, then, to prevent any photos of myself from being taken. If for some reason inspiration struck and someone produced a camera during a family event, I quietly hid behind my uncle John, who was easily wide enough to conceal a small boy. And when that annual horror known as school pictures rolled around, I just never brought the forms home. On the one occasion when my mother mentioned that she'd like an image of me, I took one of my cousin Jay, who was my look-alike, and gave it to her. Unsuspecting, she kept it on the refrigerator for years, much to the puzzlement of my aunt Pat.

Thus I rode out my adolescence and teen years safe from the glare of flashbulbs. And I escaped my college years unscathed as well, save for one unfortunate shot showing my friend James in drag, looking eerily like Bea Arthur, while I leer at a phallic-shaped balloon gripped in his hand. The negatives of this print, taken shortly before we attended a Halloween party at the local Episcopal church, are still running around somewhere and are certain to come back to haunt me at my Nobel Prize ceremony.

With that one startling exception, photos were not an issue again until I got my first and only job in the professional world. Upon my arrival at the office, I was told I needed to have a picture ID taken if I wanted, as I was assured I did, to enter and exit the building without having to be searched each time by the hulking guards who flanked either side of the one door in and out. Deciding that it would be unwise to throw a fit on my first day of gainful employment, I sat sulkily before the camera and got it over with. Thankfully, the picture was the size of a postage stamp, and it remained safely in my wallet for the entire five years I worked at that company. I shredded it the day I left for good.

I was quite pleased at myself for having made it through almost three decades without being photographed more than absolutely necessary. Of course, not having a driver's license or passport had posed the occasional problem, but then the joys of travel are overrated anyway, and staying in one place for a lifetime seemed a small price to pay for my convictions. Then, one awful afternoon, the phone rang. Never one to sense danger early on, I picked it up innocently, only to be greeted by the editor of a book I'd recently finished.

"Hi," she said airily. "We're doing the jacket for your book this week, and we need you to send over a photo."

I gave the little harmless chuckle I'd always used for such requests in the past. "I'm afraid I don't have one," I said. "Just use copy."

She was adamant. "We have to have a picture," she said, an edge in her voice. "We always have pictures of the authors."

I will not bore you with the details of the next half hour of conversation. Suffice it to say that this horrible woman, who should have never been given a job where she can viciously abuse innocent writers by threatening to withhold advance checks, would not back down. She even had the rudeness to point out that my contract specifically required my cheerful cooperation with this matter, a point I was sure to take up with my agent when I fired him later in the day. By the time I hung up, I'd agreed to hand over a suitable photo of myself by the next week, my suggestion for using the Ranger Rick photo having been soundly rejected.

Not only did I not want to have my picture taken but this was a most unfortunate time to need one. Smack in the middle of a sweltering summer, I had shaved all of my hair off a few weeks earlier. It was growing back, but it was at a stage where I looked suspiciously like a worried hedgehog. Now, thanks to the demands of being a world-famous author, the entire known universe would be able to enjoy my bad hair day.

Distraught, I called my friend Becket, who takes very moody black and white pictures of people who do not like to be photographed. Almost all of his clients are writers, and he has developed a wonderful touch with those of us who would rather rewrite an entire novel for the third time than sit in front of a camera. We scheduled a photo session for the next day. "It will be fine," he said.

It was not fine. I was crabby. I complained. I whined. But Becket was patient. He settled me on the stool and arranged my collar. He even gave me a shirt to wear after deciding that the HOTHEAD PAISAN T-shirt I walked in with was totally inappropriate. The shirt was a black polo shirt. I hate both black and polo shirts, but Becket said it was arty, and I believed him because he said it so sincerely. Besides, he promised me an Oreo if I behaved.

The session took two hours. It consisted essentially of Becket imploring me to smile and my refusing to do so.

"Just try," he said. "You'll look great."

"I will not," I said grimly. "I look ridiculous when I smile."

"Just try," he pleaded. "Please. Pretend Alec Baldwin is reading your book and finds you absolutely fascinating."

I tried. Anything for Alec.

"Okay," he said instantly. "Smiling isn't the only look. Let's try something else."

Becket took four rolls of film. By the time I left, he was whimpering softly, and I had a headache. I did not get my Oreo.

When Becket developed the contact sheets, I went back and looked at them.

"They're all the same," I said, looking at row after row of my unsmiling face.

"I know," he said. "It's amazing. How do you do it?"

I took two of the least agonized-looking photos and put them in an envelope. I sent them to my editor with a short note: "I told you so."

When I Grow Up

I was walking down the street shortly after my twenty-eighth birthday when suddenly it dawned on me: I will never be an astronaut. This is simply a fact. At my age I am too old to begin the NASA training program. Normally this wouldn't be any big deal, no real cause for alarm. But for some reason, this discovery set off a disturbing chain of thought as I realized to my horror that at some point I had quietly crossed the line where there are now many, many things I am too old to do or too far along to start learning.

When I got home, I made a list of careers that, in all probability, were no longer options for me:

Child prodigy
Someone in the 18–25 range on surveys
Teen model
Serious novelist under 30
Ingenue

Okay, so perhaps I never wanted to be any of those things in the first place. And being a certain age does have its advantages. I cannot, for example, be drafted in the event of war. I no longer have to pay outrageous insurance premiums on my car. I am almost old enough to run for Congress. But when it comes to having a career, my options are dwindling rapidly.

Remember those glorious days of youth, when everything seemed possible and nothing stood in your way? Why, I changed my future occupation on an hourly basis. One morning I wanted to be a fireman, that afternoon a doctor, and later that evening an explorer. I went through a whole week of looking forward to life as a cowboy, only to pitch it in an instant to be a Barnum & Bailey circus clown. It was a thrilling time, filled with endless possibilities and limitless horizons. When anyone asked me what I wanted to be when I grew up, I had an answer, and usually several. "But," I always pointed out afterward, "I haven't exactly decided yet." I didn't want to fence myself in when there were so many exciting options.

But all of that quickly ended sometime around my twelfth birthday. (Interesting how discovering the joys of masturbation is followed so quickly by an avalanche of unpleasant awakenings, isn't it?) While wanting to be a pro baseball player is fine when you're five, when you hit your teens people generally start expecting more from you.

I still vividly remember taking a career test in high school in which we were instructed to answer questions designed to gauge our interests. Using some odd sort of number system taken directly from a *Cosmopolitan* test on relationships, we then added up our results and plotted two points on a graph. Scattered about the graph's field were various types of careers — exciting things like architecture, biological sciences, nursing, and, most appealing of all, government. Wherever our points met on the graph, that's the field we were destined for. I feverishly found my two plot points and moved my fingers together to find which of the many thrilling futures would be mine.

Imagine my dismay when, instead of coming together on economics, veterinary medicine, or even the arts, my fingers met over...empty space. There was one small corner of the graph that remained empty, and I was smack in the middle of it. All around, marvelous careers circled like glorious, shining prizes, but they were just out of my reach. I checked my points again; they were correct. Somehow, the answers I'd given to the questions resulted in absolutely no career prospects at all. When I presented my empty, futureless graph to my guidance counselor, he chuckled wryly. "Don't you worry," he said. "It just means you have a lot of interests. You can be anything you want to." I didn't tell him that I had no idea what I wanted and had been hoping the chart would give me some hints.

Things picked up a little a few months later, however, when a military recruiter came to the school to administer the ominously titled Armed Services Vocational Aptitude Battery test, called ASVAB for short. Taking the ASVAB test was entirely voluntary, but the time it was offered coincided with gym class, which that week involved square dancing. While most of us had little interest in the military as a way of life, when time came for the test, the library was packed.

Given the amazingly grim nature of the armed forces, the ASVAB was remarkably fun. Unlike the SATs or the other standardized tests we took on a regular basis and loathed, the ASVAB involved lots of problems taken directly from everyday life. At least everyday life in the Marines or the Army. For example, one section involved looking at lists of items that might be found in a military storeroom, things like uniforms, tents, flashlights, rifles, jeep parts, and gallon jugs of mayonnaise. Next to each item — and there were about a hundred of them — was a number. Our job was to run through a list of random numbers on our test papers, find the items to which they corresponded, and write them down. We had three minutes to see how many we could match up.

Apparently, I did very well on matching up blankets (number 00789), gas masks (13986) and boots (87602), because several weeks after taking the ASVAB, I received a letter informing me that I had been recommended for Navy nuclear engineering training. I was assured that my ability to match up numbers with their corresponding items was unsurpassed in my school, and probably in the entire world, and that the Navy would give me just about anything to enlist. I was ecstatic. Finally I had proof that all of those hours playing Concentration as a child had paid off.

In the end, at the insistence of my father, I never did get to enter the breathtaking world of nuclear technology. Instead I went off to college where, set upon by the same evil people who insisted I couldn't be a clown, I was forced to pick a major. For many reasons, not the least of which was that it seemed the easiest and you didn't have to do fractions, I chose English. Even then I had no idea what I would do with my degree when I was done. I figured I had four years to figure it out.

Four years later, with nothing to show for myself but a working knowledge of Milton and a much-praised critical variorum on a Keats ode, I still had no idea. I went so far as to fill out an application for the seminary, in the vain hope that it would give me another four years to make up my mind. Throughout it all the Navy had continued to call my home during my college years to tell me there was always a bunk waiting for me aboard one of their spiffy submarines. While it was nice to have this safety net, by that time I knew there were other reasons I didn't want to head out to sea with a lot of men in close quarters besides the fact that I dislike water.

Then, one night I was driving a visiting lecturer on writing back to her home in New York City. She asked me what my plans were after graduation. When I mumbled something about not having decided yet, she gave me her publisher's phone number and insisted I call the next day. I did and subsequently got my one and only actual job in the business world. Finally, I had a direction, even if it was completely by accident. When people asked me what I did, I promptly said, "I'm an editor." The pressure was off. It stayed off for five years, at which time the company was purchased by another publisher and we were all given the option of either moving to New Jersey or being fired. Being a sensible person with no tolerance for big hair and toxic waste, I chose downsizing and was thus dumped into the world once more with no idea where I was headed.

That was several years ago, and in that time I seem to have become, by default, a writer. This is fine with me. But it seems to upset a lot of other people, to whom writing is clearly not so much a profession as it is something to do when you aren't really working. No matter that I've published upwards of twenty books and won a handful of awards or that I manage to support myself entirely on the words that come out of my head. I'm still suspect. I'm still cheating somehow. Writing is nice as a hobby, but as a career? It's as though I'm still hanging around in that empty space on the career graph, and no one is very happy about it.

This is most evident when I am introduced to people for the first time. "What do you do?" they ask politely.

"I'm a writer," I say flatly, knowing what will come next.

I get one of two responses. The first, "Have you written anything I might have read?" is the least unpleasant of the two, as it at least displays some sort of acceptance on the part of my new acquaintance of the fact that I really do this for a living. Things inevitably go downhill, however, when it is revealed that I have not written anything that has either reached the number one spot on *The New York Times* best-seller list or been turned into a television movie featuring Tori Spelling.

The second response, "Oh, a writer. I hope you publish something someday," is more typical, implying as it does that I could not possibly have written anything yet because the speaker has never heard of anyone foolish enough to admit that he actually writes for a living. It is almost always accompanied by an indulgent little smile of the sort reserved for children who have just announced that they fully intend to become Supreme Court justices or rock stars.

Even my family doesn't quite get it. "How's it going?" my father says cheerfully when he calls. "Are you still doing that thing you do?"

"You mean write?" I say.

"Yes, right, that's it. Is it working out yet?"

"Well, I just published another novel."

"Really? Did they pay you for it?"

"Not enough, Dad."

"Well, that's okay. It's always a place to start, right? You have to begin somewhere. One of these days you'll figure out what it is you want to do."

I'm curious to know what the cutoff limit is for when certain ambitions and careers become unacceptable. For example, it seems absolutely thrilling for a six-year-old to say she wants to be an Oscar-winning actress. "That's right," we say, "you keep practicing that acceptance speech." But when those same words are mouthed by a 34-year-old waitress whose biggest part to date was as a silent extra in a community theater production of *Our Town,* we tend to disbelieve them. An eight-year-old boy whose greatest ambition is to be the star of the Rangers is encouraged to bash his way around the rink. His seventeen-year-old counterpart is told to start thinking of trade school as a viable option.

At the same time, please note that we lavishly reward those who refuse to give in. Actors. Sports stars. Supermodels. All highly paid. All fawned over. All because they refused to advance beyond the age of four while the rest of us put away the basketballs and dog-eared scripts and learned how to do accounting and fix cars instead. We don't love these people because they're great; we love them because they didn't listen. You can bet their parents still call them up and want to know when they're getting real jobs.

I used to attempt to explain my work to people, spouting lists of my books and pointing out my various magazine and newspaper columns as proof of my claim of being a real, full-time writer. But that was simply too much effort. Besides, if you have to work that hard to get people to take you seriously, you're too defensive. Now I don't bother. Whenever anyone asks me what I do, I remember my five-year-old self and respond happily, "I'm thinking of being a clown, but I haven't decided yet."

Adventures Among the Straight People

Trial by Fire

As a queer man, I've made a concerted effort to stay away from that harpy of gay life — the Fag Hag. I'm referring, of course, to that peculiar breed of heterosexual woman who finds it some kind of thrill to hang around men she'll never get into bed with and who remarks frequently that spending time with her beautiful but untouchable boyfriends is just like having a pajama party with all her girlfriends, minus the thrilling conversations about tampons and armpit shaving that we men missed out on in our teens and that it can be argued some segments of our population have been making up for ever since by clumping around in glitter wedgies and dresses that would scare Gloria Swanson back up her staircase.

While some men find the company of these women amusing, I am not one of them. I grew up in a house with two older sisters, and consequently the feminine mystique was demystified for me very early on. The esoteric rituals of depilatory creams, sanitary napkins, and the appeal of a smart vinegar and water spray hold absolutely no fascination for me, and the world of straight women is one I haven't wanted to spend time in since I first discovered the joys of man-to-man sex in a men's room at the local Sears.

As a result, over the years I've carefully honed my Hag Radar to the point where I can spot clingy heterosexual women immediately and avoid them like an ex walking on the street with a new, more handsome lover. I refuse to spend a minute with any woman who begins a sentence with "If only you weren't gay," forces me to go shopping to help her pick out something for her nephew's bar mitzvah that is both tasteful and will make Stacey Schermer green with jealousy, or asks me to share oral sex techniques that will make her boyfriend babble uncontrollably and promise her emerald earrings. If I wanted to hang around a lot of straight women, I'd have a Tupperware party.

Because of this aversion, the fact that Grace and I are such good friends surprises most people. Thoroughly heterosexual (except for one drunken confession about a fantasy involving Cindy Crawford and a bottle of lemon-scented oil that I promised never to tell another living soul), Grace is one of the few straight women I know who doesn't expect me to be able to offer decorating advice. She never asks me to go to weddings with her as her "special friend," never teases me for not knowing anything about opera, and not once has she asked me if her favorite actors are gay. We met on line waiting to buy tickets to a k.d. lang concert. Each of us thought the other was a dyke.

What enables Grace and me to remain friends is that we respect each other's views. She knows not to try to make me appreciate modern painting, and I in turn have stopped trying to explain to her why hockey is the only perfect art form. Her idea of indulging in Italian food involves sun-dried tomatoes and basil-infused olive oil; mine is eating SpaghettiOs straight from the can. I cannot understand her fascination with nerdy academic men who take her to lectures on the underlying Christ figure metaphors in Renaissance sonnets. She finds my obsession with big jocks who like to go to Steven Seagal movies appalling.

Despite these differences, we have managed to stay close, and for five years this partnership has run smoothly. But a few months ago something happened that tested the strength of our friendship, and it was the last thing either of us expected.

It started when I dragged Grace to Sam Goody to look for the latest John Michael Montgomery album. She had just forced me to sit through an agonizing French movie involving subtitles that had no pronouns and featured lots of pale men and women throwing leaves at one another while weeping, all set to a score composed mostly of bassoons and what sounded like small children being crushed to death by stones. I had fallen asleep halfway through and was still aching from a persistent cramp in my left leg that made me limp around like a wounded bear. As my revenge, I had brought Grace record shopping because I knew she would hate it. As expected, she was being a pain in the ass.

"You just didn't understand it," she said as I pulled her though the doors. "It was all about how men and women relate to one another."

"Nothing blew up," I said. "There were no cute men and far too many breasts for my liking. And what was that business with the nun and the bowl of tomatoes?"

Grace snorted. "Just because Harrison Ford didn't run through wearing a fedora and fending off a bunch of natives with only his manhood and a short piece of stick doesn't mean it was stupid. Not everything is about sweating and saving the world. You know nothing about art."

I ignored her, rounding a large Garth Brooks cutout whose considerable cardboard bulge poked invitingly over a display of his latest album. "I don't know why you have to listen to this stuff anyway," Grace was droning as I pulled her down the aisle of the country section. "It's so...twangy."

"Shut up," I told her venomously as I tugged on her upper arm. "It's better than that Eurofag–Pet Shop Boys–mindless computer dance crap you listen to. And I think you need to do some more water aerobics; you're getting a little thick up here, and you'll look doughy in that off-the-shoulder thing you bought to pick up boys at the opera."

She responded by kicking me viciously right where my cramp was, so that I stumbled and lost my hold on her arm. Sensing an opportunity for escape, she made a worthy attempt at dashing back toward the jazz section while I tried to regain my balance. Fortunately, I was able to cling to a surprisingly sturdy Mary Chapin Carpenter stand-up and regained my balance quickly enough to give Grace a head start of only a few feet. Before long I was right behind her.

I had just managed to get a good grip on her hair and she was in the process of trying to step on my foot when the fireman came into view. He rounded the corner near the vocals section and made his way toward us, striding by the Anne Murray section briskly. Without a word, we paused midbattle, an unspoken truce brought on by the appearance of the only thing on earth that could get us to stop — a Fire God.

I should explain that Grace and I both have a thing for firemen. More precisely, we have an obsession with anything remotely to do with firemen. We walk the long way to the subway so we can go past the firehouse and linger while we watch the guys wash the trucks or straighten the hoses or even put the recycling bags at the curb. We always stop to pet the dalmatians at our respective houses — Highrise at mine, Domino at hers — and chat up their owners, Fireman Steve and Fireman Robert. When the fire department had a big subway ad campaign last year, we had a contest to see who could steal the most posters. STAY BACK 200 FEET means nothing to us when the sound of sirens calls.

This man fully lived up to my vision of what a fireman should be. His very broad shoulders were packed into the telltale blue fire department T-shirt, the rest of him into jeans and boots. His short dark hair begged to have someone's hands — preferably mine — run through it. He had the shadow of a beard. He was the most beautiful thing I'd ever seen. I glanced over and saw that Grace's eyes had practically rolled back in her head, and she was beginning to drool like one of those pictures of a medieval saint in ecstasy over being pierced by God.

We stared in awe as our firefighter walked through the aisles, both of us carefully searching for signs that he might be available. Whenever he passed behind a pillar or display, we held our breath waiting for him to reappear. We bobbed and ducked and scurried after him, following silently. After a minute of watching him, I surmised that there was no one near him who might be a potential significant other, and a quick scan showed that the ring finger of each hand was bare.

"It's not real," Grace murmured.

"I can practically smell the smoke," I said.

We looked at each other suspiciously. There was only one fireman and two of us. The answer to the problem was simple, and we both knew it. One of us would have to die.

"I'll invite you to the wedding," I said and started after my soon-to-be husband.

I got about five feet before a violent force knocked me flat against a display of Amy Grant Christmas CDs. In my daze, I could only vaguely wonder where Grace had learned to bodycheck like that. I felt like the casualty of a Ranger-Canuck run-in as I peeled myself away from Amy's oversize smiling face.

"Get out of my way," Grace hissed as she streaked by. "This one's mine."

Pausing momentarily to check her lipstick in a metallic theft-prevention sticker on the back of Juice Newton's *Greatest Hits*, Grace made her way across the store, softly humming "On Top of Old Smoky." She was wearing her short skirt, and I knew I was in trouble if I didn't think of something fast. My mind raced as I ran through a list of possible diversions, watching in horror as Grace moved closer and closer to my intended. Finally, when she was halfway down the aisle, I stopped her dead in her tracks by shouting, "Forget it. He's heading for the show-tunes section."

The fireman, who was in fact intently perusing that area of the store, turned around, the original cast album from *Carousel* in his manly hand. I quickly ducked behind a stack of Judds boxed sets, leaving Grace to fend for herself and congratulating myself on my cunning.

Forced to think quickly, Grace relied on her years of experience in dealing with men. "You know," she said cleverly, "I just loved *Backdraft.*" She followed this with a little laugh and a swing of her hair. The fireman smiled. *That bitch,* I thought bitterly.

Peering out from behind the Judds, I could clearly see every move Grace made. She was standing as closely as possible to the fireman, laughing at everything he said and swinging her hair thirteen times a minute. Her hand rested lightly on his masculine forearm, her nails purposefully stroking the soft dark hair as she babbled on and on, holding him captive. At that moment, I hated her more than I'd ever hated anyone in my life. She wasn't my friend; she was a husband stealer.

I had to think of something to get her away from the man I was sure I would spend the rest of my life with. Grace was working herself up into her "if you take me home I'll do things to you that you only thought were possible in European soft-focus films" mode. I'd seen it before and was all too familiar with her success rate. Unfortunately, I was too busy thinking about the fireman's hairy forearms to concentrate fully on my next move.

"Can I help you find something?" a voice asked from behind me, startling me back to the real world.

I turned around to find a store clerk watching me. I stared at his wide, innocent face and blinking eyes. He reminded me of a big, stupid dog waiting for a bone. What I did next was the act of a desperate man.

"Actually, Walter," I said, glancing at his name tag and whispering conspiratorially to gain his trust, "I'm just watching that girl over there."

Walter looked over the stack of grinning Naomis and Wynonnas with their big red hair and squinted at Grace, then looked back at me. "She sure is pretty," he said.

I put my hand on his shoulder. "No, Walter," I said seriously, "you don't understand. I think I saw her stick some blank tapes in her backpack."

Walter blinked again while his brain processed this new information. "Are you sure?" he asked, his demeanor growing bolder as the enormity of the situation sunk in.

I nodded, hoping I looked innocent and believable. Walter, eyes gleaming, pulled his pants farther up his belly and squared his shoulders. Then he walked over to where Grace was playing out her seduction scene. "Excuse me," he said politely, interrupting a gale of girlish laughter as he tapped her sharply on the shoulder, "but would you please come with me."

Grace looked as if he had slapped her. "Why?" she said defensively, her eyes narrowing. Walter, his adrenaline churning out of control from this unexpected power opportunity, turned stone-faced. "Just come with me, please, ma'am. We'll talk about it downstairs. In the security office."

I knew Grace wanted to put up a fight, especially over being called "ma'am," but she also didn't want to make a fool of herself in front of her prey. The fireman was looking from Walter to Grace, and she knew she was in trouble if she said anything unladylike. She went quietly, remarking over her shoulder to the fireman as she left, "There must be some mistake. I'm sure it will be cleared up in a minute. Don't go away."

As Grace marched past me, I avoided looking at her, pretending to rifle through some Patsy Cline CDs. She tried to stop and say something, but Walter pushed her ahead of him. "It's always the innocent-looking ones," I said, shaking my head sadly as they went by.

Once Walter and Grace were out of sight, I made my move. I knew she would be back once Walter opened her backpack and found nothing but breath mints and notes for her doctoral thesis in early English pastoral poetry. I had only a few minutes to get the job done and get Mr. Fireman of My Dreams out the door before Grace would be on the loose again. I strolled over to my beloved, my heart beating wildly as I planned my strategy.

"I wonder what that was all about," I said casually as I sidled up next to him, checking out the way his butt looked in his jeans and resisting an urge to run my tongue down his neck.

He looked over at me quickly, then looked again. A good sign. "I don't know," he said. "She seemed like a nice enough girl. I can't imagine she did anything wrong."

"I'm not sure," I said, determined to crush once and for all any positive thoughts he might have about the evil vixen who almost took my man. I was pretty sure he was playing on my team, but these days it's hard to tell, and I always end up going for the straight ones anyway. If I was going to end up disappointed, I was going to make damn sure Grace was right there with me. "I think I smelled liquor on her breath."

He looked at me again and grinned, his perfect lips parting to reveal white teeth that appeared to have benefited from years of orthodontia as a child. I thought I'd pass out when I saw the way his chin dimpled. Then, just as I was getting a good look at his beautiful brown eyes, he went back to his work. He appeared to be looking for a particular album, pawing through the stacks of CDs intently.

I know absolutely nothing about musical theater apart from the fact that at some point someone sings something, but I decided to improvise. If my man liked musicals, I could learn to like them too. Besides, I'd seen that movie where Mary Poppins dresses a bunch of kids up in curtains and takes them on a bicycle tour through the Alps while they're all pursued by nuns and eat strudel while playing the guitar, and that had to count for something. I hummed something I thought sounded vaguely show tune–like and snatched up the nearest CD without looking at it, pretending to read the back intently.

"Isn't this the show Liza was in?" I asked, throwing out the only name I could come up with that I knew might have anything even remotely to do with musicals. I saw her sing in a Diet Coke commercial once and figured she must have been in something along the way to deserve that kind of exposure.

He glanced over. "I doubt it," he said, looking at me strangely. "That's the sound track from *Terminator 2*. You must be thinking of *Cabaret*."

"That must be it," I said lightly. "I'm always getting them confused." I put it down again and wondered what he'd do if I just tackled him and threw him to the floor. Things were not going well. Then, to make matters worse, before I could come up with another conversation starter, Grace reappeared at the top of the escalator. I could see by the way her lips were set as she stormed up the aisle that whatever was left of Walter would regret the day she walked into his store. I quickly moved to the other side of the fireman so that he was between us. I knew she wouldn't risk damaging him just to get at me.

"It seems," she said pointedly as she came to a stop and rearranged her face into a mask of sweetness, "that someone made a mistake."

I tried my best to appear sympathetic. "That's terrible," I said, leaning in to smell my fireman's manly scent and noticing the hair that peeked over the collar of his T-shirt. "Some people will just do anything to get noticed."

"Some people," said Grace, shredding a CD wrapper with her nails, "are going to be sorry forever when I get my hands on them."

The fireman had made his way to the *R*'s and seemed to have found just about everything he wanted. Grace and I glared at each other balefully over his back as he bent to retrieve one last item. We both knew that time was running out, and both of us were desperate to get the man's clothes off. Now it wasn't even about him; it was about which one of us was a better flirt. Grace decided to go for broke. She brushed the hair out of her eyes and pretended to see the fireman's shirt for the first time.

"Oh, wow," she gushed, "a fire department T-shirt. What company are you with?" We both know the location of the Manhattan fire departments by heart. I held my breath, hoping he was closer to my apartment than hers.

"Oh, it isn't mine," he said. "It belongs to my brother. I would never go near a burning building. I'm in the Shearson-Lehman accountant training program."

Grace and I looked at each other, our eyes welling up and our bottom lips trembling. Our mighty fireman was a fraud. It was all a cruel joke. This was worse than finding out there was no Easter Bunny or even that Newt Gingrich was running for president. Far worse. This was as bad as finding out that the hole in the ozone layer was caused by excessive chocolate consumption.

After that, it didn't matter whether the guy had a boyfriend, a girlfriend, or a golden retriever named Jack.

He had the shirt, he had the boots, and he had the look. But he wasn't the real thing. He would never come home from work sweaty from a practice run. He would never let us wear his T-shirts around the house. We would never be able to make love on top of the hook and ladder with him wearing nothing but his heavy black boots. We both knew that, despite his looks, there was nothing exciting about tax-exempt status or itemized deductions or plant amortization and that sex on a pile of account ledgers would never be as exciting as the feeling of yellow rain gear on bare skin.

Once again, we united in our desperation.

"Look at the time," I said miserably. "*60 Minutes* is going to start soon."

"I'd better get going then," Grace played along. "I don't want to miss Steve Kroft's piece on the decline of family values."

The faux fireman waved farewell, oblivious to the fact that he had broken our hearts, and we headed off. Dejectedly, we walked out the door of Sam Goody and into the black night. Outside, we looked up at the empty sky and cursed our bad luck.

"Just think," I said after a minute in which we both contemplated our mutual loss, "we almost killed each other over an imposter."

Grace put her arm around me. "Why don't we go get a beer and laugh about it. I'll even let you drink out of the bottle instead of forcing you to put it in a glass."

Arm in arm, we headed down the street to our favorite bar. We might not have firemen, but we were content to have each other as friends. Before we'd gotten half a block, we had already started to laugh about it and were finding fault with the man we had so recently thought a god. "His nose was a little crooked," I pointed out.

"And that single-eyebrow look isn't for everyone," Grace added thoughtfully.

Then we spotted the hunky policeman standing next to the subway entrance, handcuffs gleaming seductively against his thigh. I could feel Grace stiffen next to me as she thrust her chest out to maximum advantage, and her arm slipped from mine. This time I wasn't giving her any chances.

"Well," I said cheerfully, breaking away from her. "I think it's time to ask directions to somewhere."

As I dashed toward my God in Blue, I heard Grace's heels clicking on the pavement right behind me.

Singing a Different Tune

When my nephew, Jack, was about to turn ten, I called my sister well in advance of the actual date and asked her what he would like for his birthday. The tenth year is a big one for any child, marking a transition between the dreamlike world of kick-the-can and paper dolls and the horrors of adolescent life like spontaneous erections and big bullies named Kurt, and it should be commemorated accordingly. I still recall vividly the gold eagle pendant my cousin Jay, my childhood hero, presented me with on my tenth birthday. I wore it religiously, until one sad day the clasp snapped and it was lost forever, improving dramatically my choice of accessories but leaving me cheerless. I wanted Jack to have such a moment to remember.

Karen knew instantly what Jack would cherish above all else on this earth. "CDs," she said promptly. "He's really into music now."

This was good news. Children as a rule have no taste whatsoever, so when buying music for them, it's just a matter of going to the record store and picking up whatever is hovering at number one for that given week. Even if they have no idea what it is, kids will play it loudly and thrash about in some semblance of dancing, feeling very grown-up and pleased with themselves. The week of my tenth, it was the sound track to *Grease* burning up the charts, and I received it with delight and some surprise, considering that my mother had forbidden me to actually see the movie after learning that the word "shit" was uttered freely. I played it endlessly (taking Olivia Newton-John's solos, naturally), and to this day I wonder how my life would have turned out if, instead, AC/DC or Bruce Springsteen had ruled the airwaves in the fall of 1978.

"So what should I get him?" I asked. "Hootie and the Blowfish? Coolio? Maybe Garth Brooks?"

Karen laughed. "Oh, no," she said cheerfully. "Nothing like that. He likes sound tracks."

"Great," I said, visions of *Grease* filling my mind. "So maybe the music from *The Lion King* would be good." I had this vague notion that every ten-year-old thrilled to all things Disney.

"Actually," Karen said, "he wants the albums from *Cats* and *Les Mis.*"

I was speechless. I wondered if my sister had any notion of the implications of what she had just said. Maybe, I thought, I'd just heard her incorrectly. "You mean the Broadway shows?" I asked doubtfully.

"Yep," she confirmed. "He loves those. We went and saw a touring show of *Cats,* and he's been humming the songs ever since."

I didn't know what to say. This was my sister talking, the one whose only response to my coming out was "Well, you know I'm okay with it, but God says it's wrong, so you're probably going to hell." Now she was telling me, in effect, that her very own son was exhibiting early signs of becoming a raging queen. And not only did she not seem to mind; she was enthusiastically supporting his bid for queerdom.

Okay, I know the stereotype of the gay man singing show tunes is one many people find offensive. I know I don't happen to like them very much. And we all go out of our way to reassure kids that just because some boys like ballet and some girls like softball they aren't necessarily going to end up with rainbow flag stickers on their Volvos and mineral water in the fridge. But really, when's the last time you saw a little boy who could belt out "I'm Just a Girl Who Can't Say 'No' " grow into a fascination with Pamela Anderson Lee's breasts? Can you blame me for being suspicious?

Still, I knew I had to be careful. I certainly didn't want to out the kid to his mother, especially so near to his birthday. If he really was tripping gaily on the heels of Dorothy's ruby slippers, I didn't want her to freak out, which I knew she would. She was already worried about the effect it might have on him being raised by a single mother, and she'd probably go out and buy him a rifle to compensate. She still harbors a suspicion that I'm gay because our father never built a tree fort with me.

"Um, Karen," I said, trying to determine exactly how serious the situation was. "Does Jack just kind of hum the music, or does he know all the words?"

"It's amazing," she said ingenuously. "He knows every word to every song. He hears them once and has them down. He can even do the motions Grizabella makes when she sings 'Memory'. You should see it; it almost makes me cry. Why?"

"No reason," I said casually. "I'll see what I can do."

I hung up and ran to the record store. Now I'm not saying it's right to actively hope that a young child is gay, and far be it from me to suggest that we push those showing the slightest indication of a queer aesthetic along in any way. All I will say is that I skipped with a glad heart to the show-tunes section and snatched up Jack's requested discs. For good measure, I added *Phantom of the Opera* and briefly paused at *Gypsy* before deciding that would be too much even for me. He had to be broken in slowly.

Once home, I wrapped the CDs and shipped the whole mess off to my sister with a prayer to the Patron Saint of All Young Queens — Charles Nelson Reilly. On Jack's birthday, I called to see how things were going.

"Hello?" Karen shouted when she picked up the phone. In the background I could hear the swelling tones of "Music of the Night" filling the apartment.

"Hi," I said briskly. "How's the birthday boy?"

"Just great," Karen said. "He's absolutely thrilled with the CDs. You didn't have to send so many, you know."

"That's okay," I said. "You only turn ten once. What's that shrieking?" In the background I could hear what sounded like a recent castrato bemoaning his fate.

"He's singing," Karen said proudly. "All morning it was 'On My Own' from *Les Mis*. Now he's learning *Phantom*."

I tried not to crow in triumph. "That's really great," I said. "He'll be a singer in no time." I imagined what my sister would think when Jack started renting Joan Crawford movies. She'd probably blame it on me, but I didn't care. Score one for our side.

"Oh, he already is," Karen said. "You should hear him try to do 'Evergreen.' "

This was more than I could stand. "He sings Streisand?" I said incredulously.

"Oh, yeah," Karen answered. "He's been getting into my Barbra records since he was six. In fact, my present to him was his own copy of *The Broadway Album*. We sing it together."

I had to hang up.

So maybe ten is a little young to know for sure. Still, I think the fact that I asked for an Easy-Bake Oven when I was seven was probably some kind of early indicator, sexist or not, of what would come. My friend Anne agrees. She gave her Barbie a crew cut and rechristened her Alix when she was four. Now Anne drives a UPS truck and plays rugby for her wimmin's collective team. You can't ignore the facts. Jack's birthday is coming up again, and this year he wants to visit the Smithsonian to see the exhibit of first ladies' gowns. Karen say she's glad he's showing such a healthy interest in American history.

Homo Improvement

I love working around the house. Blame it on some rogue butch gene roaming my system, probably the same one that periodically commands me to watch baseball or have an overwhelming desire to buy a pick-up truck. Whatever it is, I find that I am constantly doing things like rewiring the outlets, replacing the grout in the bathroom tiles, or installing faucets with spray attachments to the kitchen sink. I freely admit that I don't always do these things well, but I do approach them enthusiastically, flinging open my how-to books with abandon and going at the old wallboard with my trusty hammer and a merry heart. At the moment, every window in the house is covered in shrink-wrap plastic to increase energy efficiency, and I have a half-formed plan to put built-in bookcases in the office.

Naturally, my favorite place to indulge my obsession with all things handy is hardware stores. I love them and find myself wandering helplessly inside whenever I pass a particularly fine one. There's just something about a well-ordered collection of hand tools, gardening implements, and fasteners of various types that can fascinate me for hours, even when there's nothing in the store I actually need. If the place also carries lumber, I'm lost in rapture as I inhale the scent of freshly sawed pine and envision a Sunday afternoon constructing a deck.

My favorite hardware store of all is Home Depot. Not just any old hardware store, Home Depot is the Valhalla of home improvement centers. It floats majestically in a concrete parking lot sea, calling to the thousands of do-it-yourselfers who flock there from morning till night, drawn by the siren song of circular saws and the magical lure of easily assembled kitchen cabinets. Like enchanted heroes in a Norse legend, weekend carpenters and professionals alike follow the beacon of the twenty-foot-high orange letters that make up the Home Depot sign. "Come to me," they beckon seductively. "I am the promised land."

And indeed it is. My first visit to Home Depot was nothing short of a religious experience. A cavernous space, it is crammed from floor to ceiling with every conceivable hardware, gardening, and plumbing product. I had gone there for a simple screwdriver, but by the time I wheeled my cart to the checkout line several hours later, I had also picked up such indispensable items as a butane fireplace starter, new wallpaper for the bathroom, assorted lengths of nylon hose, iris bulbs in various colors, and a tool of which I had not even the vaguest notion of its use but that leapt unbidden into my arms as I passed by. Such is the magic of this wondrous place.

Nor is the appeal of Home Depot limited to the items that can be purchased there. Not the least of its charms is the large number of attractive young men who work there. Invariably clean-cut and hunky, they are all clearly designated by their festive orange aprons and by the fact that, at least here in Boston, they are all named Tom. The Toms swarm all over Home Depot like ants

over a fallen peach, appearing at regular and often-star-
tling intervals to say hello and ask if they can be of service. Surprisingly, they actually do seem to know where
things are and how much they cost. Once I decided to
test a Tom who had asked me four times if he could help
me. Picking up a wicked-looking piece of PVC, I asked
Tom to explain it to me. For the next fifteen minutes, he
entertained me with a demonstration of how one could,
by using the remarkable PVC device, change one's ordinary kitchen sink into a cunning garbage disposal.
Impressed, I bought two.

Despite their allure, the Toms are not what fascinate
me most about Home Depot. What I find even more
interesting is the enormous number of queer men who,
like me, seem to spend hours roaming the aisles. Home
Depot is cruisier than any bar I've ever been in, and this
despite the unflattering fluorescent lighting that falls from
some nether region far overhead. At any given time, the
place is crawling with fellow homos looking for everything from geraniums for the summer house to real
Italian marble for the bathroom floor. Yet neither the host
of actual repairmen, plumbers, and carpenters who do
business there nor the Toms seem at all fazed by sharing
their Palace of Masculinity with a bunch of queens. I've
often wondered if they don't recognize the gay men in
their midst or if they simply don't care.

A few months after my first visit, I had occasion to
find out once and for all just how clued-in the Toms
were. One Thursday evening I made a happy trip to
Home Depot to fetch some padding to lay beneath the
host of tasteful yet affordable Oriental rugs I had recently purchased there. In a hurry to get there and back, I
had written the measurements of all the rugs on the

back of the nearest piece of paper. In this case, it happened to be an envelope that had contained a letter from my friend Hank.

Paper in hand, I entered Home Depot's whooshing doors and made my way through the electrical wiring, past the paint shakers, and down the flooring aisle. There I discovered roll after roll of handy backing just waiting to be cut into perfect sizes for my rugs. All I needed was a Tom to help me. Luckily, one popped up not two seconds later, asking if he could be of use. When I said he could, he seemed genuinely glad, unlike young men whose job it is to ask such questions at, say, Macy's, where an answer in the affirmative is likely to result in an hour of petulant and reluctant service.

Tom and I selected a hefty roll of serious-looking padding and rolled out a length of it in the aisle. It was a beautiful thing, thick and cushiony, and it made me happy just to see it. We then stood there, hands on our waists, looking down at it as we shared a moment of common manliness. We were about to embark on a home-improvement journey together, one that would require both strength and cunning, and when it was all over we would have accomplished something useful. In that moment I understood the appeal of the football huddle.

"Beautiful padding," Tom said, nodding his head approvingly.

"Sure is," I answered. "Looks sturdy too."

Thus invoking the Hardware Gods, we got to work. Tom produced a handy utility knife from his back pocket, and we set to work hacking up the padding. I took out the paper with the measurements written on it and handed it to Tom. He studied it carefully, as though basking in the glory of my penciled eight-by-fours and ten-by-fives, the numeric language of the lumberman.

Then he turned it over, and my heart sank. Hank is a very clever man. Among other things, he makes his own stationery, paper included, and decorates it with a wide variety of amusing pictures and stamps. On the back of this particular envelope, where it had been sealed, was a giant pink lip print stamped in fluorescent ink. I tried to remember if Hank's name had been on the return address but couldn't recall. I wondered if Tom would even notice.

Tom looked at the lips, then grinned. "A love letter, eh?" he said teasingly. "Is she a real Betty?"

I thought seriously about this. Certainly Hank has many appealing qualities, and I'm sure his boyfriend of many years thinks he's just swell. Yet I doubted that he was what Tom would consider a real Betty. As I saw it, I had two choices: I could go along with him and say that no, it wasn't a love letter and she was just a friend, or I could come out and announce that yes, he was a real sweetheart and wasn't it wonderful that so many different kinds of people shopped at Home Depot. Either one would require an explanation I wasn't sure Tom would understand.

Beyond that, I wasn't sure I wanted to shatter the illusion of male bonding we had created there on the floor of Home Depot. I know, I know...it's important for us all to expand the horizons of our straight friends whenever possible. So sue me. Gay men don't get a lot of opportunities to be just "regular guys" in the world of lumber and nails, and it was sort of fun running around such an *über*-butch place blending in. Like Cinderella, I wanted the ball to go on a little while longer before Tom turned into a pumpkin and my fairy godmother took away my tool belt.

I looked down at the envelope and said a silent apology to Hank for the betrayal I was about to commit. "Not so much a Betty," I said to Tom. "More of a Mary."

"A Catholic girl," Tom said, nodding sympathetically as he began to cut pad. "I know how that is."

A Model Queer

The phone rang at 9:30 on a Friday night. It was Stephen.

"Hi," he said cheerfully. "What are you doing tomorrow afternoon?"

I hate questions like that. Having been given no actual information on which to base a decision, I have no idea how to answer. And the risk is high. Should I say I'm busy, it inevitably turns out to be something I really wanted to do, like go to a Bruins game, and I then have to pretend to have looked at the wrong date on my calendar. If I say I'm free, I have unfailingly agreed to participate in something dreadful, like being dragged to a foreign film festival, and I am forced to invent, on the spot, some believable commitment I'd momentarily forgotten about.

Because I am not particularly good at lying under pressure, this often puts me in a difficult position. Once, after having innocently said I was free for Tuesday night and then being told that, in that case, I was accompanying my friend Alice to an eight-hour performance of Japanese opera, I tried to get out of it by saying that I'd just realized I was having my wisdom teeth out that afternoon.

"That's funny," she said evenly. "Didn't you have them out the night we were supposed to go to the

Peruvian puppet festival too? I guess in that case you wouldn't be interested in the extra tickets I have to the Garbage concert on Friday. Bye."

With that unfortunate incident in mind, I decided to go for the middle ground with Stephen. "I'm not sure," I said vaguely. "I have a manuscript due Monday, and it depends on how much work I get done on it. Why?"

"I'm doing this shoot," he said. "It's supposed to be about lust, and I want you to model for me at a strip joint."

"I am not stripping for a national magazine," I told him firmly. "My father might see it. My publisher might see it. Anyone might see it."

"Don't worry," he assured me. "You'll just be sitting at a bar watching strippers. All you have to do is look horny and stick money in their G-strings every so often. No one will even know it's you unless they look hard."

That certainly sounded easy enough. Too easy. "Why me?" I asked suspiciously.

"I need an all-American type," he said. "The magazine wants a mix, and you're the most clean-cut guy I know personally."

"You mean I have the shortest hair."

"Yeah. So, can you make it?"

My first reaction was to say no. Having my picture taken is far from my favorite pastime, and avoiding that very situation is something of a mania of mine. I was about to say I just didn't think it was a good idea and hang up.

But before I could open my mouth to decline Stephen's request, I was suddenly overcome by a vision of my face on magazine covers across the country. Me surrounded by hunky men wearing nothing but lots of oil and the smallest of briefs over their bulging crotches. While I am usually not one to have delusions of grandeur, I found myself swept up in the indulgence. After all, it isn't every day that writers get a shot at fame.

"All right," I said. "Where is it, and what time?"

Stephen told me to show up at 2 and gave me directions to the club. The next afternoon, I dutifully dressed myself in my one and only suit, as Stephen had said he wanted the models to look like Wall Street brokers. There was a brief moment of ugliness when I couldn't button the pants, which I hadn't worn in almost six years, since my one and only job interview. But I held my breath and got them closed, all the while thinking bitterly about lost youth. I hoped I wouldn't have to pick anything up.

I managed to find the club with no problem. It was a splashy-looking place in the heart of the financial district, the windows tinted black and a length of red carpeting stretched from the entrance like a lascivious tongue. There was no sign, and I felt slightly deviant as I walked toward it. Warily eyeing the burly bouncer outside, I went in and made my way to the back. Sure enough, three models were having their pictures taken by a photographer. Three female models. With nothing on but bikini bottoms.

"Can I help you?" one of them asked me, her hands on her hips. "Uh...no," I stammered, trying not to look at her breasts. "I'm waiting for someone. But I'll just wait out front." I beat a quick retreat before she took anything else off.

I don't know why, but the thought that it would be female strippers I was posing with had simply not occurred to me. I knew Stephen was straight, likewise the

magazine he was shooting for. But the image of me surrounded by naked women is not one I am generally
accustomed to envisioning. If I am going to be lusting,
the object of my affections is not likely to be wearing
spike heels and pasties. I'd just assumed that the strippers
would, well, not have breasts.

Once safely back outside, I stood with the bouncer
and watched the hookers working the block, trying to
decide if I should just go home before I got into any
more trouble. Across the street a woman walked up to a
Jeep waiting at the stoplight. She pulled her top down
and laid her breasts on the hood, as though presenting a
cut of meat for inspection. Just then, a police car came
around the corner, lights flashing. The woman took off
down the street, her breasts flying wildly, her purse
under her arm as she set the land distance speed for the
fifty-yard dash.

As the woman turned a corner and disappeared, a
cab pulled up to the club's door. I was so busy watching
the fleeing hooker that I almost didn't notice Stephen as
he got out with another man, camera bag in tow. "What
was that?" Stephen asked. "The Olympic trials?"

He introduced the man with him as Ed, another
friend he had roped into the day's festivities. Ed had hair
much longer than mine, and he hadn't shaved in a few
days. He was, Stephen explained, supposed to represent
the underside of corporate lust. I didn't ask what I was
supposed to represent.

Before we went in, I cornered Stephen. "You didn't
tell me this was a straight club," I said accusingly. "Do you
know how many naked breasts there are in there?"

He just grinned. "I must have forgotten. Look, how
hard can it be to look excited? These girls are beautiful."

"Oh, right," I snarled. "When was the last time you got hot and bothered watching a Mel Gibson movie?" He ignored me and went over to say hello to the strippers.

Stephen set up his equipment at one end of the room. Because it was still early, there were only about fifteen men in the club. They all looked like someone's father, only slightly more rumpled. They quietly sipped drinks and watched the women, who danced on an island in the middle of the circular bar. The men's eyes were fixed on the gently swaying breasts floating above them, as though hypnotized by their movement. I tried to see what they saw, but the thrill escaped me entirely.

For the first shots, Stephen wanted Ed and me to sit at the bar, as though we were relaxing after a hard day on the trading floor. He asked one of the women to dance directly in front of us. Ed and I were directed to look up at her rapturously as she ground her hips and puckered her red lips seductively. I obligingly gazed upward, wondering how she managed to balance in high heels while avoiding knocking over the drink glasses and ashtrays that lined the bar for effect. I hoped the puzzled look on my face would pass for burning passion.

"All right," Stephen said after a few minutes of shutter snapping, during which I'd counted the number of moles on the dancing woman's legs. "It's time for the money." He handed us each a wad of one-dollar bills. "Now, when Sarah bends down, run your hand up her leg and slip a dollar in her garter."

Ed grinned. "This should be fun," he said. I gulped my fake drink, wishing desperately that it were real.

Sarah started dancing again, and Ed and I commenced lusting. The sound system was blasting Blondie's

"Heart of Glass," and every time Deborah Harry surged into the chorus, Sarah would crouch down and either Ed or I would run a hand up her leg and put a dollar under the black garter belt around her thigh, until she had a whole fan of bills covering her leg. When we ran out of bills, she gave them back and we started over again.

We repeated this routine with a number of different women, sliding our hands up various thighs and fumbling with one garter after the next. "Ooh, ooh, ooh-aah," Debbie crooned, and we maneuvered another dollar up another leg. Ed seemed to be enjoying himself, and the women were very pleasant, if somewhat bored. I did my best to appear inflamed by them, but I was really thinking how oddly hairless their bodies were under my fingers.

Stephen then asked two of the dancers to do some one-on-one shots with us. I was paired with Karen, a beautiful woman with long wavy hair and big brown eyes. Stephen gave me a cellular phone, and we pretended I was showing Karen how to use it while she hung on my every word. We pressed buttons and made the lights go on and off, telling each other terrible jokes while trying to appear seriously horny. In the meantime, Ed was being mauled by the woman he was posing with. She was sitting on his lap and running her long-nailed hands through his hair.

During a pause in the shoot, Ed's partner noticed his wedding band. "What would your wife think about this?" she asked teasingly.

"She knows it's for art," Ed deadpanned. "Otherwise she'd kill me."

Karen looked at me. "And what would your wife think?"

"I don't know," I said. "But my ex-boyfriend would probably be very surprised."

I waited for her to rush away and start shrieking a Homo Alert. Instead, she laughed. "You mean all the guys over there watching us are getting hard-ons wishing they were you, and you couldn't care less?"

"Ironic, isn't it?" I said helplessly.

She smiled evilly. "Well, in that case, why don't we give them something to really get off on."

The next thing I knew, she grabbed me by the tie and pulled me up off my barstool. While I did my best to breathe, her hand went around my neck, and she pulled me toward her. Suddenly, her tongue was in my mouth.

Now, there are women that I find attractive. And from time to time I've looked at various women and wondered what it would be like to make love with them. But it's always in a very general, nonexplicit kind of way, sort of like you'd look at a BMW driving alongside you and wonder in passing what it would be like to ride in, even though you probably never will. I had certainly never had the urge to grab a woman and make out with her. Now, purely by accident, I had my chance to find out what it was like.

Karen was beautiful. She was funny. She was a good kisser. She had a lot of the qualities I would find attractive in a man. Except that she was a woman. I tried to feel insanely hot for her, but all I could think about was that her lips tasted like peppermint.

The moment was shattered by Stephen saying very loudly, "I am telling every single person you know about this. And I have the film to prove it."

Karen let go of my tie. "Anything happen?"

"Sorry," I said. "Maybe if you had a beard."

Stephen wanted to take some shots of the dancers in their dressing room, so he left Ed and me to wait for him at the bar. As we sat there, one of the men who had been watching the shoot came over to talk to me.

"You sure got it good," he said sadly. "I'd pay fifty bucks to have one of them do that to me."

I looked at him. "Well," I said consolingly, "some guys have all the luck."

Separation Anxiety

Shortly after my twenty-second birthday and a few months before my parents' thirty-fifth anniversary, my phone rang at 11 at night. It was my mother. My mother hasn't been awake after 8:30 for at least twenty years, so this came as something of a shock.

"Who died?" I asked, since I could think of no other reason for her to be up and talking to me at that hour.

"No one," she said. "What do you think of your father?"

"What?"

"What do you think of your father? I mean, as a husband?"

"What are you asking me for? I'm not married to him."

She sighed. "I'm not in love with him anymore."

To be honest, her announcement was not the surprise it might seem to an outsider. Children generally know when their parents are unhappy together, and my sisters and I had been aware of it for many years. We just assumed that neither could be bothered to find anyone else he or she liked any better. Still, she was my mother, and even though I was aware of the issue, I hardly wanted to discuss it with her. After all, this was the woman whose idea of talking about sex was to leave *The Marriage*

Guide for the Christian Woman in my sisters' rooms shortly
before their weddings. Since there was apparently no
companion guide for men, I got all of my ideas about sex
and marriage from this helpful book, and for years all I
could remember was the haunting paragraph suggesting
that during the first attempt at intercourse with his wife
a man should stop for a minute after penetration and try
to calm down so that he wouldn't ejaculate from overex-
citement. When, upon my own first sexual experience
(which admittedly involved slightly different genders,
orifices, and positions), I discovered that this little trick
failed to work, I was sorely disappointed.

Given this shaky background, I was not enthusiastic
about the possibility that my mother might now decide
to discuss with me, in depth, my father's shortcomings in
the marriage area.

"Oh," I said helplessly. I was about to suggest that she
call someone who could be of more help, like her sister.

"I want to leave him," she said before I could proffer
that recommendation. "And I want to marry Rod."

This is where things began to get interesting. First of
all, Rod was the pastor of my mother's church. Not only
was he about twenty-five years her junior, but he was also
married, with two small children.

"You can't do that," I pointed out, ever practical.
"Rod is already married." As far as I was concerned, the
matter was settled and we could all go back to bed.

"He's leaving his wife," she answered. "He's telling
her now, and we're leaving tomorrow for Vermont."

Then it all came out. She wasn't thinking of leaving
my father; she had already done it. In fact, she and Rod
had been having a passionate affair for months.
Apparently, Rod's secretary had found out and threatened

to expose them to the church congregation, thus bringing things to a head. Despite myself, I was sort of impressed. I knew she'd been the head of women's ministries at her church, but I had no idea she had thrown herself so fully and completely into her duties.

Still talking in a steady rush, as though afraid I would interrupt her and spoil the whole thing, she said she knew Rod was the man for her because, unlike my father, he went to church and he prayed.

"Well, he sort of has to," I said. "I mean, he is the minister and all."

She ignored this bit of wisdom and informed me once again that in the morning she and Rod were leaving for Vermont, where apparently they were going to set up house immediately. "What do you think of that?" she asked finally.

What do you say when your mother, whose most spontaneous action to date has been changing her haircut of thirty years, informs you that she is leaving your father for a man of God? "Good for you," I said, trying to remember what all the self-help books said to say when confronted with sudden and unexpected news. "As long as you're happy." Then I recalled what she said when I came out to her and couldn't help adding. "But I just want you to know that I still think the Bible says it's wrong."

When she hung up, I immediately called my sister Karen, who at the time lived in the same town as my mother. "What the hell is going on?" I asked. "Is she insane?"

"Don't ask," she said. "She's driving me nuts. Now I know how she felt when we were all in high school and she hated the boys we dated."

"What has Dad said?"

"He doesn't know yet," Karen said.

Until that point, I'd forgotten that my father was away in Burma on assignment for the government. He'd been there almost four months and wasn't due back for another six weeks.

"Didn't she call him?" I asked incredulously.

Karen sighed. "She says she sent him a letter."

As it turned out, my mother never did send that letter. In the end, it fell to Karen to tell my father what had happened when he called a few days later for his twice-weekly check-in. By then, my mother and Rod were happily ensconced in a house in the Green Mountain State that they had bought with the money my mother cleaned out of the bank accounts. When informed of all of this, my father's response was similar to mine. "Oh," he said, then asked how the dog was doing.

When he returned home a few weeks later, my father was oddly cheerful. Assuming he would need some company, and secretly dying to know what he thought about it all, I went to visit him. He looked happier than he had in all the time I'd known him. In fact, he didn't even have time to say hello when I arrived. "I have a date," he said, rushing out the door with a wave.

I later found out that after my father learned of my mother's leaving with Rod, he did two things. First, he had his wedding band cut off, since over the years his fingers had grown and it no longer slipped off easily. Then he made a list of the women he wanted to date when he returned home. He was now busily engaged in working his way through that list. Since neither of my parents had dated much before they married, they were both apparently doing as much as they could to make up for lost time.

Several days after my arrival, my father received in the mail a letter from my mother informing him that she was coming back at the end of the week to pick up some of her things. The letter contained two lists. One of the lists was composed of the items my mother intended to take from the house. It was a long list, taking upward of five or six pages. In it, my mother displayed an uncanny ability to recall accurately the contents of every closet, cupboard, cellar, box, drawer, and chest in the entire house. She even listed, individually, all the items of the junk drawer in the laundry room.

In condensed form, it went something like this:

Furniture
Artwork
Carpets
Kitchen utensils
Cookware
Books
Garden tools
Photo albums, minus pictures of Dad and his relatives
Silver
Christmas tree ornaments
Croquet set
Piano
1 cat to be determined

The second list contained the items my mother had decided my father could keep. It was a far shorter list and looked something like this:

Grill and charcoal
Wood in woodpile
Hay in barn
Snowblower
Dog
1 cat to be determined

A few minutes after reading the lists, my father left the house and went into the barn. We had no idea what he was doing, but we thought it better not to ask. When he returned a few hours later, he was in a decidedly better mood but refused to tell us what he'd been engaged in all afternoon.

On the appointed day, my mother arrived precisely at 10 with an enormous U-Haul van and her sister to help her load it. Rod himself was nowhere to be seen. For the next few hours, they busily emptied the house of most of its contents. As they carried out lamps and boxes and rugs, my father stood looking on, a delighted smile on his face. He didn't say a word as my mother hauled away the accumulated debris of thirty-five years.

When my mother finally finished, she closed the back of the U-Haul, hopped in, and trundled off without so much as a good-bye to my father. Catching her reflection in the side mirror, I could see that she had a very self-satisfied look on her face as the truck turned onto the road. When I looked over at my father, he was grinning madly.

"What's so funny?" I asked.

He started laughing. "Did you see those big cardboard boxes? The ones marked 'dishes' and 'garden stuff'?"

"Yeah, why?" There had been about ten very large, very heavy boxes that my mother had gone to great lengths to get onto the truck. In fact, she had left out the piano she'd planned on taking just so she could fit them on.

"Well, I put those there," my father said. "They were all filled with bags of horse shit from the barn."

This is the fun part of divorces that happen when everyone is older: You see sides of your parents that you never knew existed. And because you're no longer a child and have long ago stopped believing that your parents are madly in love, you can, for the most part, enjoy it because it has absolutely nothing to do with you. The months following the separation were filled with all sorts of incidents, accusations, and general anxiety as things were hammered out, but they were always good for a laugh or two. My mother, for example, lost her first two lawyers to heart attacks, one right after the other, dramatically proving what I had suspected all along about her effects on those who worked for her. I also discovered that my father was much funnier than I had ever expected. He immediately took to calling my mother The Wicked Witch of the North and announced that now that she was gone, he no longer had to endure a house that smelled of potpourri.

Much to my surprise, my mother and Rod lasted. Although unable to work any longer as a Baptist minister, Rod found a challenging position as the manager of a pizza parlor. As for my father, in the end he never made it past the first name on his list of women. After dating number one for several months, he informed us that they were getting married. My mother, too, announced her impending nuptials shortly after the various divorces involved were final. My sisters and I were ecstatic on both counts, mainly because since both of the new spouses were considerably younger than Mom and Dad, we wouldn't have to worry about looking after them when they became aged and infirm.

Things didn't work out so cleanly for everyone, however. My nephew, Jack, was forced into a peculiar position. Rod's two little boys were Jack's age and also happened to be his best friends. Now, because of my mother's marriage to Rod, they suddenly rocketed from the status of friends to that of uncles, which confused Jack enormously. "Look at it this way," I said at the wedding as he tried to puzzle out their new relationship, "Now you have two more people to borrow money from when you get older."

Cyberslut

A fter years of trying and failing miserably, I have finally become what I aspired to be in high school — a slut. It's true. No one I went to school with would ever recognize me now. Overnight, quiet, innocent little me has turned from a good boy who cleaned his room into a raging nymphomaniac who ties men to beds, takes on three at a time, and has absolutely no limits whatsoever.

All right, so maybe I had to compromise a little to make my dream come true. I admit that the action isn't always exactly as realistic as I'd like. And there is the little matter of my having to become a woman.

It all started the day I innocently decided to check out some of the chat rooms on my on-line service. Signing on and breezily clicking the talking-heads icon that beckoned coyly on the menu bar, I was whisked away into a room where a group of friendly people were talking about their pets.

"What do you feed your bulldog?" asked someone called TashaBarks, and almost immediately several helpful souls responded with their suggestions for kibble amounts and vitamin additives guaranteed to produce a shiny coat. *This is fun!* I thought and began scrolling through the other rooms available. Plant lovers. Football enthusiasts. People who cooked artichokes. It seemed that everyone, in what was no doubt a direct influence of the redoubtable Virginia Woolf, indeed had a room of their own.

That's when I saw it. Tucked away in the corner of my screen was a little, brightly colored button. "Private Rooms," it said ominously, like some discrete sign in a hotel catering to mobsters. "Private Rooms"? I had no idea such a thing existed in cyberspace. I wondered what they could be. Never being one who could resist even the smallest of temptations, I moved my mouse furtively across the screen. I hovered over the button for a moment, pausing expectantly while I made my decision. It was a little like the feeling I used to get whenever I'd find where my parents had hidden the year's Christmas presents and I'd sit looking at them for several minutes, agonizing over my choice. Inevitably, I'd reach for the first one and start shaking.

Of course I gave in and clicked the button. Then I waited while the screen whirled and re-formed until once again I was greeted by a list of rooms. But unlike the harmless pet people and chipper marigold growers of the first chat area, these rooms were populated by a slightly less savory crowd with decidedly prurient tastes. In fact, there were dozens of dens of iniquity to choose from, with names like hairychestedm4m, bicuriousmarried-men, and str8collegemen4gays. It was just like shopping for my own personal fantasy.

I immediately felt slightly guilty, a holdover from the days when I firmly believed that both Santa and Jesus saw my every move. Then, intrigued, I selected a room that sounded promising — hardjocks4u — and entered. To my delight, I found myself in the company of twenty-three other users. The room was filled to overflowing with ready, apparently horny jocks. I sat back, threw off my cybertowel, and waited for the locker room to heat up.

But during the entire time I remained in hardjocks4u, nothing happened. The dialogue screen featured a lot of people typing things like "Who's hard here?" and "Anyone in Toronto?" but no one ever answered. And despite the appealing personal profile I'd created for myself ("Likes Baseball! Ready Now!") not one person asked me if I wanted to hit a few balls with him.

Bored, and feeling slightly rejected, I signed off. I couldn't believe that with all of the horny computer users out there, I couldn't find one who found me worth even a "Want to play coach?" come-on. Then I had a thought. As me, I hadn't had any luck. But maybe on-line sex was like real sex. Maybe I just needed to be someone more interesting.

Thus was born Nikki. Nikki is 23. At 5 feet 3 inches tall and 103 pounds, she cuts quite a figure, especially with her long red hair and green eyes. A design student in New York, Nikki's favorite things are rough men, alternative rock, and sushi.

I suppose I could have made up a male character, but somehow doing that felt like cheating. Improving upon myself just to get laid seemed, well, creepy, like having pectoral implants and getting my teeth bonded. This way I got to be a whole new person, one with no background. It was like playing a character in a television show. I just pretended I was guest starring on *Melrose Place.*

Nikki made her debut in badboyz4naughtygrlz on a Friday night. Within seconds, she was bombarded with six instant messages from men who found her absolutely thrilling. Every few seconds a bell would ding and another little dialogue box would appear on my screen with a message from some admiring suitor. "Hey Nikki!" said one, "Want to get oral?" "Do U like big 1s?" asked another.

After a few moments of giddy confusion, I figured out how to work the little boxes and went searching for Mr. Right. It wasn't easy. Nikki was turning out to be more popular than I'd imagined, and every time a new message box opened, the one I was writing in would get shoved off to the side and I wouldn't be able to find it again.

Besides, for each person who contacted me, I had to take a minute and look up his personal profile to see what I was getting. I weeded out people who had no profile at all (probably FBI agents), put down slogans from the '70s for their quotes ("Keep On Truckin' " was surprisingly popular), and anyone who said he looked "like an older Mel Gibson/Kevin Costner/Richard Gere." (All three are attractive, but really, how well will they hold up?)

I finally settled on a man whose handle was JackNOff. His profile informed that he was 34, an "account executive," and "into ladies who know how to party." His instant message had said, "Want to sit on it?" All right, so maybe he was the cyber version of the used-car salesman at the bar with his shirt collar open to his waist and the distinct odor of Old Spice hovering around his head. But he sounded ready. I had no idea Nikki was so easy. But she insisted on talking to Jack before I could stop her. What can I say; it's just the kind of girl I am. Apparently.

"Hi, Jack!" Nikki typed back briskly. "I'd LOVE to sit on it."

"Kool!" Jack fired back. "It's 8 inches with big balls!"

It soon became clear to me that everything that appeared on the instant message screen was required to be followed by an exclamation point, as though the sender was constantly in a state of near orgasm and could barely find the time to misspell common words. It was all so thrilling I had to close my eyes and take a few deep breaths before going on.

"Wow!" Nikki responded, amazed by her luck. "I bet it would feel REALLY good in my pussy!"

"Sure would!" Jack informed me. "What's your pussy like?"

This took me aback. I hadn't really thought about my pussy before. I wondered, if I indeed had one, what it would look like. I tried to recall the pictures I'd seen in *Penthouse* when I was eleven, but my recall wasn't very clear. "Shaved," I said finally, unable to think of anything else.

That's when Jack popped The Question. "Are you a real girl?" he asked.

I thought about this for a moment. Maybe my pussy answer had been unsatisfactory. Did women shave their pussies? I wasn't sure. Besides, I thought, was it right to fool Jack into thinking some hot gal was on the other end of his dialogue box, pussy at the ready? Maybe I should just end it right there. Then I pictured hundreds of men across the country, their wives sleeping unsuspectingly in the other room while they typed dirty messages to girls they'd never get in real life. In solidarity with those sleeping wives, I typed my response.

145

"Hey — I have a hot, shaved pussy, don't I?"

To my amazement, this seemed to satisfy Jack. "Great!" he answered. "Let's do it!"

Nikki and Jack did it. So did Nikki and BigDkinNY, Nikki and SailorMan, and Nikki and BadDad. Nikki did it with everyone who wanted her and in every way imaginable. And as she did, a pattern began to emerge. First of all, it appears that every single man on the Internet stands six feet tall, weighs 180 pounds, and has an eight-inch cock. It also seems that, to a man, they are willing to do anything suggested to them by a 23-year-old with a filthy mouth.

"I want you to stick your fingers up your ass!" Nikki told BadDad (43, balding, into home brewing), and he did.

"I want you to sit there in your chair and watch me get fucked by my boyfriend!" she informed CopStud (36, Italian, drives a pickup), who was happy to oblige.

"Then I want you to suck my pussy juice off his dick!" she tossed out, despite Cop's earlier pronouncement that he "didn't like fags." To her delight, he was more than willing, and I felt I'd scored one for our side, even if it was only on a computer screen. "His cock tastes SO GOOD," he cooed, and Nikki wondered about the wife and three children mentioned in his personal profile.

After eight straight hours of fornicating in cyberspace, Nikki was exhausted. She'd sucked, fucked, spanked, whipped, bitten, and shaved her way through a dozen men, each of whom had told her she was the hottest sex they'd ever had and asked if they could meet her in person. Laughing lightly, she declined, saying she had to wash her hair (so many men had asked to come in it, it would take hours). Sated, and feeling very naughty indeed, I turned the computer off and went to bed.

I lay there for a while, chuckling at the joke I'd pulled on a bunch of straight guys who were none the wiser. I wondered what they would think if they knew the person getting them off had a dick. I pictured SailorMan (40, divorced, likes schoolgirl uniforms), who had asked Nikki to tie him up and spank him. Thinking of how he'd enthusiastically typed "I'm cuuuuuummmmmmmmmiiiiinnnnnnggggg!" in response to Nikki's head-giving capabilities, I wondered what he'd do if, at the crucial moment, she'd written back, "Surprise! My dick is bigger than yours! Have a nice day!"

Then, just before I fell asleep, I had another thought. An unsettling thought. If I was having such fun being someone else, perhaps I wasn't alone. Maybe there were others who, like me, just weren't who they said they were. I thought of RuffPup (28, tattooed, rides a Harley) and how he'd tied Nikki to his bed and made her beg for it before savaging her repeatedly. Suddenly an image came into my mind. Two dykes in Toledo. Bored with the *Murder, She Wrote* rerun. Sitting at their keyboard.

"Hey," says one, sipping her Diet Coke and rearranging her flannel nightgown, "this one sounds hot. Nikki. She likes sushi!"

"Perfect," says the second. "Watch this." She sends Nikki a note reading, "Bend over, I want to shove my big dick up your sweet ass!"

Nikki's reply comes back: "Sure, Ruff! I love it in my butt!" The dykes collapse in gales of laughter and start typing.

The Way I See It

No Splashing
in the Gene Pool!

There's been a lot of talk recently about the possible existence of a gay gene, some little bit of nelly DNA traipsing down our bodily pathways like some out-of-control subcellular fairy godmother who taps her glittery magic wand and turns some of us into queers. Apparently, just as we can inherit from our parents poor eyesight, male pattern balding, or an inability to clot successfully, we can now have passed along to us a fondness for Ethel Merman, an inexplicable affinity for Volvos, and a penchant for going antiquing in Vermont on fall afternoons. Now, while I'm all for expanding our knowledge of this fascinating little world we call the human body, I'm not at all sure I approve of this latest scientific foray into my inner workings.

Before going further I would just like to say in the interest of full disclosure that I am hardly impartial on this topic. I freely admit that I think it's entirely irrelevant. I really don't care why anyone, myself included, is gay. If you want to believe you were born to love other boys, hurrah for you. If you insist that you're challenging socially restrictive gender roles by actively choosing to munch muff, I say munch on, sister. If you're one who has concocted complex theories about nature working in conjunction with nurturing, I say your time would be better spent watching *Xena: Warrior Princess.* It matters not to me. If you really demand an answer, I propose that the same aliens who created Easter Island and crop circles are responsible. After all, who else but queers would think of decorating a barren shoreline miles from nowhere with gigantic festive tikis?

But I do seem to be among the minority on this one. There are a lot of people — both gay and straight — who demand more empirical evidence for the existence of same-sex desire. Much like the seekers of knowledge banging their way through the South American jungles looking for the Nine Insights revealed in James Redfield's *The Celestine Prophecies,* these questing souls want desperately to know where this fabulous state of queerness originates from. For these folks the source of sexual attraction is a puzzle of intense fascination, and they look for answers in hard science. To them the possibility of pinning a queer gene under a microscope is the modern-day equivalent of at last finding the elusive Holy Grail.

And what an eclectic group these earnest wonderers are. First and foremost, we have the throngs of queer women and men for whom being given any definitive reason for their sexuality would be welcome relief. Long bullied by others, or perhaps simply beset with good, old-fashioned religious guilt, these people are simply unable to just get over it already. Haunted by memories of being called "drama club fags" and "softball dykes" in middle school, they ache to know once and for all that it isn't their fault. "See!" they want to cry out in triumph to disapproving families as they wave the latest issue of *Scientific American.* "I can't help it. It says so right here in black and white. With charts."

And let us not forget the anxious parents themselves. What a boon such a discovery would be to them. A gene to hang it all on would certainly eliminate all those hours of wondering if not enough time was spent playing catch, or perhaps too much emphasis was put on neatness and table manners. Having something concrete to point the finger at would make it seem more like being part of a club, like parents whose children have MS or cancer and who gather together for support. "Oh, yours has it too?" they could say reassuringly to other mothers and fathers whose children were similarly afflicted, free at last from the burden of having caused it themselves. Of course, there would still remain the small question of how that little bit of biological data got inside us in the first place. But never mind; it's a start, and at least we could still blame it all on Mom and Dad when the going gets too tough.

Ironically, perhaps those for whom the discovery of a gay gene would be most agreeable are those who already hate us on general principle. At last, something to explain it all away. Why, we aren't so scary after all. We're just defective. And because that rascally gene is tucked away safely inside us, there's no chance of its spreading to uninfected people through casual contact. What a relief!

Surely once this gene were isolated, a vaccine of some sort wouldn't be far behind, or at the very least a test that would indicate early in pregnancy if a fetus carried the awful gene. (And hey, maybe all that talk about outlawing abortions was just a bit premature, don't you think?) One little blood test, and problem solved. Saving future generations of children from the curse would be only a matter of minor surgery, freeing up a lot more time for fretting over racial minorities, unwed mothers, and Hollywood.

Maybe we could even have telethons, like the annual bash Jerry Lewis throws for his kids. Some second-rate celebrity could become our spokesperson — Phyllis Diller might be good, or Sally Struthers now that her correspondence-school gig has ended. One weekend a year, she could take over our local PBS stations and hold a variety show to raise funds for getting rid of this terrible pestilence. I can just imagine her wheeling out children cursed with the horrible gay gene. Holding them up to the camera, she would speak in pleading tones of the awful life awaiting them unless a cure could be found. Dollars would pour in as willing Americans pledged their dimes and nickels to eradicate once and for all what would become the newest birth defect. Instead of perverts, we would be a cause. Undoubtedly, some enterprising soul would come up with yet another colored ribbon (aubergine, perhaps?) for celebrities to wear to show their concern for our plight while accepting awards.

Then again, maybe there are more practical uses for a gay gene. We could, for instance, manufacture it in mass quantity and use it as a biological weapon. Specially equipped Fag Fighters would spray Agent Pink over war zones. Within a matter of hours, the unsuspecting soldiers would all find themselves overcome by the need to redecorate. Throwing down their guns, they would stampede to the nearest Bed, Bath & Beyond, where they would put aside their petty differences and unite in their mission to create a beautifully accessorized Laura Ashley bedroom. Peace would reign planetwide.

But that's all in the future. What about now? What about those who have already been affected? If the fact that I adore Bette Davis can be blamed on a piece of pro-toplasmic fruit salad in my basic makeup, what does it mean for the gay youth of tomorrow, the ones born in the last few years and already too old to be fixed easily? I'll tell you what it means: BOCES. Let me explain.

Where I went to school, in the oh-so-progressive wilds of upstate New York, we had a thing called the Board of Cooperative Educational Services, BOCES for short. In theory, BOCES was a nice idea — students who might not be what you would call college-bound would spend a part of each day at the BOCES center, where they would learn practical skills with which they might support themselves following graduation or, more likely, after dropping out when becoming pregnant or impreg-nating someone else.

Each day after homeroom, the BOCES kids would file onto special little buses and be taken away to be apprenticed in their chosen trades. Unfortunately, the BOCES offerings were limited primarily to cosmetology and automotive repair, girls choosing the former and boys the latter. The classes, which focused on such intriguing subjects as the best way to feather hair and the swift rebuilding of carburetors, were far from challenging, and those of us who were more academically inclined, but generally smaller and more timid, delighted in taunting our vocationally oriented classmates by screaming "Bye, botards" out the windows as the buses pulled away. It may not have been kind, but it was our only revenge. And they were, after all, different. "You're so BOCES," implying as it did a phenomenal level of stupidity, was the worst insult in our little social world.

Now, imagine if you will a bus idling outside your average junior high school. Waiting to board is a small group of students, say about 10 percent of the total school population. The boys stand, books clutched to their chests, discussing their recently purchased cardigans. The girls, more casually attired in jeans, T-shirts, and motorcycle boots, are combing their hair and smoking. While in many respects they look just like everyone else, there is something about them that sets them apart from their classmates. They aren't drooling or limping, but something just isn't quite, well, *normal*. When the doors to the bus open, these students plod on glumly and find their seats. The bus pulls away, and as it leaves the school parking lot, a group of students calls out, "Bye, queertards." The kids on the bus cringe in shame.

These are the kids with the gay gene. Not retarded, nor even the more politically correct "differently abled," they are instead labeled "orientationally challenged." While their handicap is not severe enough to prevent them from being mainstreamed with normal children, they do require special classes that meet their unique needs. So for a part of each day, they are shipped off to a nearby school, where the process of helping them overcome their uniqueness takes place.

Fortunately, since the discovery of the gay gene there has been a swift movement to teach educators how to handle the needs of these children. Now that their problem has been recognized as just another physical handicap, lesson plans have been made and ways of teaching them to deal with their differences have been honed. Flashcards are implemented. Phonics are explored. After years of such education, many queertards are able to lead perfectly happy lives among their normal neighbors, where their presence allows the community to feel that they are highly advanced in their ability to forgive the unfortunates their disabilities.

But that comes later. For now, the boys are taken to one part of the building, the girls to another. For the boys, the afternoon consists of learning how to sit with legs spread wide and the best ways to take up more space than necessary, followed by instruction in speaking loudly, thinking of themselves as the most important people in the universe, and enjoying interminably long viewings of team sports. The girls, after being shown numerous episodes of *Beverly Hills, 90210* featuring a shirtless Jason Priestley, are drilled in the finer points of wearing skirts, appreciating the joys of makeup, and being happy with less. The classes are hard, but the promise of acceptance helps the students to persevere. After all, they are told repeatedly, they are simply helpless victims of their degenerate nucleic heritage.

With luck, the queertards will soon learn to see their disability as simply another obstacle on the road to becoming productive members of society. If not entirely normal, they can at least be assimilated. Sure, the other kids back at school might not always be kind, but special ed has prepared them to deal with being social outcasts, and they always have each other.

The highlight of the school year is, of course, the prom. For this lovely event, all of the gay gene boys are required to invite a gay gene girl. Frilly dresses in unnatural colors are the rule for girls, short hair and pressed shirts for the boys. Music is provided by a Carpenters tribute band. Kool-Aid and Nilla Wafers add a festive touch to the converted gym, which has been decorated in a manner befitting the theme: Change Is Good.

Eventually, of course, there would be a cure for the gay gene. Slowly and surely, the last remaining holders of the queer strain would die off, making gays and lesbians nothing more than a footnote in medical textbooks of the future. Like smallpox and the bubonic plague, queerness would be eradicated, rendering special ed for queertards unnecessary and making everyone happy except those who would lament the absence of really stylish designer dresses, women's golf, and popular culture. Until then, it looks like we'll all be riding the little bus to school.

Games People Play

The last time I visited my nephew, Jack, we spent the entire time on the couch, battling each other in a heated bout of Mortal Kombat. This clever video game, which was the subject of no small controversy when it first appeared, involves two combatants going at each other in a variety of martial arts. In addition to normal abilities such as throwing, kicking, and blocking, the different players one can choose come equipped with a multitude of interesting skills, including the ability to jolt an opponent with electricity, spit deadly venom, wield a razor-sharp fan, and (my personal favorite) deliver a crushing fist into the genitals of male characters. (I tried using it on one of the two female fighters; it didn't work.)

The object of Mortal Kombat is, naturally, to kill your opponent, the more viciously the better. With each blow delivered, blood splatters across the screen, until eventually someone loses. When one player lies dead, the other can reach down and rip out his or her heart, holding it aloft in all its dripping glory while uttering a victory scream. It is all very thrilling, and the game is enormously popular, particularly with the under-twelve set. Apparently they do nothing else but practice it for hours. Jack, who is eleven, wielded his joystick with amazing dexterity, slashing and hacking away at me, his beloved uncle, while I tried futilely to figure out how to duck. Within seconds Jack was waving my heart over his head, grinning madly.

My angelic, loving nephew then turned to me and delivered his own fatal blow. "You suck," he said.

See, this is the problem: Games today are mean. And as a result, children are growing up mean. Instead of living life as fun-loving sprites sledding down hills and skipping rope, they are fast becoming bitter little creatures who measure their success by how many hearts they can rip out. They mature into gloomy teenagers, and eventually they become mean-spirited adults and are loosed upon the world. This is not just a random thought caused by my loss of life and self-esteem at the hands of someone whose voice has yet to change. It is scientifically accurate. Bear with me; I have proof.

Once upon a time, there were kind, gentle games like jacks, hopscotch, checkers, and hoop rolling. Like the times during which they were played, these games fostered the notions of joy and carelessness once associated with not being old enough to drive or shave. Free from the anxiety caused by having to excel, children who played them grew up happily and became things like schoolteachers, inventors, and Marie Curie. They might have wanted to be the schoolyard marbles champion or the best double-Dutch jumper on the playground, but in the end it was all in fun. Rarely were noses bloodied over whose kite swooped the most elegantly or whose toboggan ran the hill the fastest.

But the years wore on, not always smoothly, and as the world changed, so did the games. Things became a little more difficult with the introduction of more complicated playthings like Twister, Barbies, and Slinky. Suddenly, the stakes were raised. Social status was determined by who could get the most Barbies and assorted accessories. Who could stand the longest with left foot on blue and right hand on green became a mark of prowess discussed at great length during recess. Whose Slinky was slinkiest was a matter of public record. Faced with the need to improve or be left behind, children became more focused, more competitive, and thus we have things like accountants, dental hygienists, and Newt Gingrich, who I understand once balanced with both right hand and foot on yellow for three hours at a friend's fifth birthday party.

Still, things weren't that bad. The board game reigned supreme, and innocent pastimes such as Candyland, Uncle Wiggly, and Chutes & Ladders filled rec rooms across the country. These were fun games, where nothing really bad ever happened to anyone. Even if you got stuck in Marshmallow Swamp, there was always a helpful friend to pull you out and send you on your way with a smile and a pat on the back. While it was always a thrill to win, playing was what was most exciting — moving the pieces around the board, throwing the dice, choosing a card. In fact, when climbing the ladders and sliding madly down the chutes ended, it was sort of sad.

But then came the '60s, when despite the peace and love flowing freely throughout the land, Americans realized that unless they shaped up, they wouldn't be the smartest or strongest kid in class anymore. The Russians had already sent a dog into space, and all we had to show for ourselves was San Francisco, paisley, and Andy Warhol. If something wasn't done — and soon — the entire country was going to be held back a grade.

Children's games answered the challenge to save America's youth, and soon the shelves of Toys R Us were overflowing with action-oriented creations like Operation and Mousetrap. Unlike their predecessors, these games were hardly soothing. To the contrary, they required a level of proficiency and cunning that sent even the most ferociously competitive six-year-old into hysterics.

For those of us born into this madness, life was harsh indeed. Who can forget holding those oh-so-realistic tweezers that came with Operation and trying to remove the patient's funny bone? Up it would come, the gleaming metal sides of the opening seemingly closing before our very eyes. Yet the patient's life was at stake, and his fate was in our hands. We'd seen hours of *Emergency* and *Adam 12,* and we knew what we had to do. Calming ourselves, we focused on the delicate task at hand. Then, just when we thought we were free and clear, a sudden twitch of a muscle ended it all. The plastic nose glowed alarmingly red. The buzzer screeched hatefully. Completely unnerved, we screamed and had to go sit quietly with a washcloth over our forehead while we recovered from the strain and admitted failure.

Mousetrap was no better, despite the ingenious Rube Goldberg apparatus that made it so popular. After spending sixteen hours setting up the game, we had to sit and watch while our gaily colored mice trudged on to their inevitable doom. Even worse, we had to execute them ourselves, turning the handle of the starting mechanism and watching helplessly as each stage of the trap was set painfully in operation. The boot kicked the bucket. The ball rolled out and down the steps. The little man dove into the pool. Finally the trap rattled down, imprisoning our squeaky game pieces and leaving them to who-knew-what horrible fate. No wonder so many of us grew up to need Prozac.

Think about it. Our favorite games in the '70s all involved imminent demise. Kick the Bucket. Don't Break the Ice! Rock-Em Sock-Em Robots. These games weren't about having fun. They were all about blame, all about survival of the fittest. Instead of having to come up with new solutions or creative answers, we had to be content to simply avoid screwing up. Winning at Don't Spill the Beans had nothing to do with skill or cunning. You simply had to stay out of the way, feeling the tension build up until some other unfortunate soul tipped the scales and finally you had someone to point the finger at. Watching any group of children playing these games, we should have seen the whole S&L scandal brewing.

Then there was the worst of all — Perfection. Even the name was ominously Big Brotherish. Oh, how well I recall that devilish little box with its oddly shaped holes waiting to be filled with corresponding plastic pieces. And all of it running against a timer. Once the clock started ticking, it was a frantic race to fit each object into its hole. At first it seemed okay. The pieces seemed to be going in smoothly. But when the fifteen-second point was reached and a pile of pieces still awaited placement, things reached fever pitch as you vainly attempted to squeeze everything into any available space. And then, inevitably, came the moment when the timer buzzed and the pieces were sent flying up into your face, an inescapable sign of failure and humiliation. Unable to attain perfection, we were forced back to less challenging games, and we never forgot it.

Then, just as it looked like we might escape our childhoods relatively intact, the video age dawned. I recall vividly the day my friend Paul got an Atari. It played only Pong, and we spent hours moving the little bar back and forth, watching delightedly as the ball pinged and ponged across his television screen. For a moment it seemed that games were fun again. My friends and I spent an inordinate amount of time in places like Chuck E. Cheese's, popping quarters into machines. Even the games where things had to be destroyed, like Centipede, were relatively harmless. When the centipede bit the dust, it simply exploded in a blast of brightly colored dots. No blood. No hearts. Just happy little pixels bursting across the screen in rainbow colors. And there was always another centipede right behind it.

But it wasn't to last. Pong gave way to harsher fare involving killing or being killed. Soon, two-player games were introduced, and the fight was really on. Now we could battle each other in real time through our Ataris. Sure, we'd played games like tag and hide-and-seek for years, and certainly capture the flag and kick the can were anything but cooperative. But now we could actually kill each other without legal retribution. Once we had the taste of blood, we became hooked. While knocking off aliens in Asteroids was fun, and even noble, knocking the crap out of our friends in Joust was completely gratuitous, and much more fun. It was a new era, and it resulted in things like investment bankers, studio moguls under thirty, and Steve Jobs.

I suspect there's about a twenty-year gap between the introduction of certain games and their direct results upon American society. In the '50s we had jacks and hopscotch — in the '70s we had Jimmy Carter and the

Carpenters. In the '60s we had Sit-and-Spin and Hippity Hop — in the '80s we had Duran Duran and *Dynasty*. In my time, the '70s, we had Operation and Don't Break the Ice! — in the '90s we have downsizing and Nirvana. No one can tell me these things are coincidental. I think it just takes that long for the effects of the games to manifest themselves. Those of my generation who mastered the labyrinthine rules of Dungeons & Dragons are busily paving the way to a new tomorrow; those of us who were never able to outsmart Simon sit stupefied as we gaze at our computers dully and wonder what went wrong. In fact, I think it's a safe bet that Courtney Love probably sucked at Ants in Your Pants and has been paying for it ever since.

It will be interesting to see where the Mortal Kombat Generation takes us. I'm not sure I want to know. Today's toys are downright scary. While games like Chutes & Ladders can still be found, more and more they're pushed out of the way by bigger, louder, more aggressive toys until all they can do is cower on upper shelves hoping some grandparent will rescue them from the jaws of the Street Shark action figures. Even Barbie and friends have had to butch it up, transforming themselves from empty-headed beach bimbos in brightly colored swimwear who cruised around in the camper into suit-wearing, briefcase-carrying Corporate Takeover Ken and the deadly Ninja Action Skipper.

As an experiment, I bought Candyland and took it to my friend Ellen's house one afternoon. Her eight-year-old daughter and six-year-old son were happily blasting away at each other with their Mighty Morphin Power Rangers laser guns. When I opened the game and started to set it up, they ran over to see what it was.

Encouraged, I quickly taught them the rules, and we started to play. Things went well for about five minutes. Then Sarah decided to push Morgan's little cardboard boy into Bubblegum Falls so she could sneak by him and get to the Gingerbread House first. He responded by knocking her solidly into the Lollipop Forest and kicking her under the table. From there it was all downhill. Snatching up their weapons, they went storming through the house with Sarah screaming, "I'm going to rip your head off, you twisted little freak!"

I'm a little frightened: She says she wants to run Disney when she grows up.

A Sporting Chance

E ach morning from May through September, as my dog, Roger, and I go for our daily walk around the nearby public pond, we are treated to the spectacle of dozens of people standing on the shore staring blankly into the water's rippling surface. They wait, slack-jawed, for something to happen, looking suspiciously like the enraptured throngs who gather around religious icons that have been reported to weep real tears.

They are, of course, fishermen. And they are *always* men. Interestingly, I have never heard even the most ardent feminist demand that the word be changed to *fisherpeople*. This is because, with I'm sure some notable exceptions, generally only men are prone to this particular form of mental illness. Who else would get up before the sun for the sole purpose of standing around for hours doing absolutely nothing and calling it a sport? Can you blame anyone for choosing voluntary exclusion from such a group?

Because there are so many of them spaced at equal intervals around the pond like living garden gnomes, I have a lot of time, as Rog and I traverse the roughly mile-and-a-half path, to observe and think about what the fishermen as a race do. Normally I would be wary of such people, just as I tend to stay away from those who speak loudly or who insist on building their own patios. But for some reason I find the fishermen fascinating, much as I do those wonderful Discovery Channel programs about the tribes in the rain forests who manage to catch wild pigs using a length of twine and unusual berries. My daily exposure to these sad people has left me with some decided opinions about sportsmen in general, which I feel it is my duty to share, in the hopes that my revelations will prevent another generation of innocent young people from becoming trapped by this peculiar addiction.

If you ask me, fishing is not really a sport at all. The word *sport* implies the utilization of some kind of skill, such as coordination, strength, or speed. At the very least, a sport should involve jumping over something, running very quickly for some reasonable distance, or having to get an object from one side of a vast area to another while other people attempt to stop you. Where's the skill in throwing a hook loaded with tempting bait into the general vicinity of lots of perpetually hungry creatures with brains the size of mustard seeds? You might as well go to a playground, scatter M&M's around, and club to death the first four-year-old foolish enough to approach, believing innocently that such treats are readily available in nature. Yet not only do the fishermen actually club the four-year-olds; they then sit around and gut them while talking loudly to one another about how difficult it was to achieve such a feat, as though they had somehow used years of study to cunningly break through the elaborate security systems their prey had constructed to thwart them.

No, fishing is not a sport. Perhaps it could be if one of the aforementioned criteria were somehow incorporated. For example, if the fisherman had to run after the fish instead of merely reeling him in from the back of a boat, or if while a fisherman attempted to cast there were seven other fishermen hurling good-size rocks at his head. Then it might be interesting. But in its traditional form, it is merely stupid.

"But what about fly tying?" some of you might ask. Surely fly-fishing deserves some respect. After all, it's a centuries-old tradition, the secrets of which are handed down from practitioner to practitioner in hushed voices. Granted, there is something elegant about this oft-lauded trade, and I suppose it does involve some measure of coordination to bundle up a lot of bits of feather, fur, and sparkly things to make something a trout will eagerly want to give its life for. But given that the same men who boast proudly of their fly-tying accomplishments are often the first to go into shock at discovering their sons working up a smart beaded evening dress, I can't be all too enthusiastic about them. Besides, never have I seen a fisherman capable of performing a credible lip sync of "It's Raining Men" while wearing one of his own creations and flinging a boa seductively around his head.

No, fishing is not a true sport. Baseball, which is a real sport in my book, involves one team of players doing battle against another group of players with potentially the same level of intelligence. Even hockey, in which intelligence is not always assured, requires the players to balance on ice skates while smacking each other about. The fisherman, who even I will admit is probably smarter than the fish he chases after, needs only to stand there and wait. He can, in fact, even drink beer while waiting. In my opinion any activity during which you can enjoy a beverage is not a sport. It is a party.

This brings us quite naturally to hunting, which is simply fishing in the woods as far as I'm concerned. In fact, hunting may be even stupider than fishing, for while the fish are admittedly confined to a relatively limited area, at least they have the benefit of being hidden by water, making their capture dependent at least partially on luck. Animals in the woods have no such luxury, being generally larger and slower. And while fish actually have to bite a hook to be caught, thereby playing at least a small role in their own deaths, animals in the woods merely have to get in the way.

It has been explained to me that men enjoy fishing and hunting because it is a way for them to feel that they are (1) superior over animals and (2) that they have provided for their families and are therefore good men. My response to this is to point out that no man I know, no matter how facile his hunting skills, is in any way mentally superior to a dog who decides that 2 A. M. would be a wonderful time to go outside for a walk and manages to get his way. Just look at a sleepy-eyed owner, bathrobe askew, being dragged down the street by a wildly happy labrador who's gotten a bonus outing by whining continuously for three hours and tell me who's the smarter of the two.

And if men want to feel that they are good providers, why can't they learn to scour the aisles at A&P in search of groceries? Not only does that activity not take up an entire weekend but it seldom necessitates the purchase of a cabin in New Hampshire or the donning of truly offensive camouflage ensembles and hip boots. In addition, I think it is safe to say that successfully negotiating a store crammed with hostile shoppers and woefully unhelpful sales clerks, only to wind up in the one

170

checkout line where the trainee needs to call for the key after every entry, takes far more patience and willpower than, say, blowing the head off of a grouse as it eats its breakfast.

My friend Bob, an avid fisherman, says that I am a hypocrite in this matter. He argues that there's no distinction between going out and catching a fish or hunting a deer and buying a salmon filet or package of 80 percent lean ground beef. In fact, he insists it's far more honest to kill something yourself than to pretend that somewhere in the world there exist cows that at a certain point magically disintegrate into hamburger patties and half-inch-thick London broils without the unpleasantness of slaughter.

I am a fair person, and I will concede that meat is meat and fish is fish, regardless of origin, and I probably wouldn't eat either one if I had to kill it myself. But I can't help but feel, however delusional it may be, that handing over ten dollars for a lovely piece of tuna ready for the grill is just a teeny bit more civilized than camping out for three days and peeing in the bushes to achieve the same thing. Besides, somehow paying for it makes it feel more like an honest trade, whereas just going out and killing the animal in its own home seems merely mean-spirited and hostile.

I have not come to my opinions on these issues easily, mind you. I grew up in an area of the country where fishing and hunting were not simply encouraged; they were mandatory. The opening days of both seasons saw the halls of my country high school empty as every able-bodied boy flocked to the river or the woods in search of blood. For weeks the lunchroom fairly bustled with boasting about rack size and fish weight, and woe unto

the child who hadn't had his first kill by the time he was
into grade school.

Of course, I suffered for my refusal to bring down a
buck or land a bass. The butt of many jokes, I endured the
taunts of my peers as I sat eating my peanut butter-and-
jelly sandwiches while they feasted on roast venison and
smoked trout they'd caught themselves on those days
when they'd skipped class to hunt while I sat inside dutifully learning geometry. But I remained true to my convictions, insisting that my lunches tasted all the sweeter
for being free from the taint of murder. My arguments
convinced no one, but, like Gandhi, I kept on, knowing
that one day I would be proven right.

In these more enlightened times, as vegetarianism
and kindness toward all living things flourish, fishing and
hunting seem to be declining in popularity. At the same
time, I've begun to notice a strange new publicity campaign being waged for these pseudosports. This spin-doc-
toring, clearly brought to us by the same clever people
who turned cotton candy into a health food by plaster-
ing "fat free" across the package, reaches out to a new
audience and involves marketing fishing and hunting as
meditation exercises. *Zen Fishing* proclaimed the cover of
one book I spied at my local New Age store; *Hunting
With the Inner Child* beckoned another.

Intrigued, I glanced inside and read for a bit. The
essential premise of these books is that the hunting of
animals, be they aquatic or earthbound, is really the physical acting-out of the search for inner peace. The animal,
be it a trout, a bison, or a lion, is symbolic of our untamed
nature. By tracking it down and killing it, we are facing
our greatest challenge, and in winning over the animal,
we win over our own fears and inhibitions. As such, dili-

172

gent practice of either hunting or fishing can, in fact, lead
to the attainment of enlightenment.

This is an interesting theory, and one I was willing to
consider as part of my path to deeper understanding.
After all, it is true that many of our daily activities are in
some ways connected to our inner workings. My meditation practice had already proven that time and again. So
on my next trip to the pond, I decided to do some
searching of my own. Borrowing a fishing pole from my
neighbor, I set out on a journey of discovery.

I approached a gentleman who was standing quietly
near a tree, his eyes trained on a bright bobber some
twenty feet away. I tried to imagine him as a Buddha
focusing his mind on a single spot.

"Good morning," I said. "How goes the search?"

"Huh?" he said.

"Have you found your inner self?" I asked.

He stared at me blankly. "Are you a ranger?" he said.

"No," I reassured him. "I was just wondering if
your daily communing with nature had yielded any
revelations."

"I caught a perch yesterday," he said brightly. Then his
face fell. "But nothing today."

Undaunted, I set myself up near a fallen log.
Opening the plastic container of bologna I'd been assured
by Bob was the favorite food of fish everywhere, I spiked
the hook through a piece and prepared to cast. Roger
looked on warily, I'm sure wondering why I was throwing a perfectly good piece of bologna into the pond.

After several failed attempts, I finally managed to get
my hook and the accompanying bologna settled into an
area near the fallen log. Holding my pole, I sat down and
began to soak in the experience. I had to admit, it was

peaceful sitting there with the sun shining down and the water gently lapping at the shore. Perhaps, I thought, I've been looking at this all wrong.

I felt a pull on my line. Suddenly, I was hit with a surge of adrenaline. The hunt was on. I jumped to my feet and began to crank the reel. It was me against the fish, and I was determined to win. I was gripped in the fist of raw nature, and it felt fine! Just like Hemingway's Old Man, I was coming face to face with my destiny. I turned and turned the reel, bringing the struggling fish closer and closer to me. Several times he rallied, pulling toward the middle of the pond, but again and again I brought him back. Finally, I pulled my prize, dripping and thrashing, from the water. It was, I think, a sunfish. Impaled on the hook, it nonetheless managed to perform an intricate series of gymnastic moves, flipping itself all over the bank of the pond. As Roger and I attempted to still it, I embraced for a moment the thrill of victory. I had, in fact, caught my inner fish.

I did eventually catch hold of the creature, primarily because Roger sat on it. Holding it up, I watched it attempting to breath, it's mouth opening and closing as it fought to stay alive in an unfamiliar element. Perhaps, I thought, in the fish's death I would come that much closer to my own enlightenment. Maybe what I gained would make up for the loss of its comparatively smaller life.

I tried to think of the fish as a teacher imparting an important lesson. I imagined it speaking to me of life and death and all of the things the author of *Zen Fishing* had written of. Just as a yogi imparted the secrets of the body or the tai chi master revealed the power of moving a single finger in a precise manner, I attempted to see the fish as another of my life's instructors. But try as I might, I had a difficult time picturing my meditation guide flopping around on his cushion gasping for air while I throttled him soundly and took one step nearer to nirvana.

Having learned his lesson, my inner child took the fish off the hook and threw it back.

Just One
of the Girls

My first summer living in New York, I couldn't wait for the annual Pride Weekend to come. I moved there in the spring, and as the days became warmer, I started counting down to the last weekend in June. After years of having no contact with a gay community, suddenly I was going to have a whole weekend devoted to all things queer. I scanned the *Pride Guide* carefully, making lists of things I thought would be fun to do. Parades. Rallies. Performances. Dances. They all went onto the list, and I was careful to balance the gratuitously decadent happenings with the more socially responsible events.

My guide that first summer was a lesbian friend from work named, appropriately, Mary. I knew very few gay men at that point, and Mary was hooked into the gay world in a way that I wasn't. She shepherded me around to the various events and made sure I saw everything. On Sunday she announced that we were going to what was supposed to be the crown jewel in the Pride Weekend crown — the annual dance on the Christopher Street pier. Mary was very much into dancing and the club scene, I was intrigued by the idea of mostly naked men, and she thought the pier dance would be a great way to indulge both our interests and allow us an opportunity to enjoy a couple of hours with our shared community.

Well, she was wrong. When we arrived at the dance, we discovered that Mary was one of only a handful of women present. Because the music sounded bearable, and because we had laid out twenty bucks apiece, we stayed. During the two or three hours we were there, my friend was treated to a continuous stream of hostile looks and sometimes outright abuse. More than once a dancing beauty would take a break from posing and come ask Mary if she was a "real" girl. Instead of feeling part of a community, she felt like an intruder. The only "pride" that seemed to be going around was in showing off the results of hours spent at the gym and under tanning lamps. The experience was ruined for both of us, and I vowed never to attend another dance.

The next year when Pride rolled around, I wasn't too enthusiastic. By then I'd had my fill of bars and clubs, one-night stands, and handsome men with empty minds. With just one rotation of the seasons, I'd decided that gay New York was a sorry place indeed. I decided that I'd sit Pride out and do something really fun, like sleep.

Then some friends invited me to join them at a women's dance that was being held as part of the Pride festivities. Now, it's a long-standing joke among my friends that I make a better lesbian than I do a gay man. I haven't seen *The Wizard of Oz* since I was four. I own every k.d. lang, Indigo Girls, and Melissa Ferrick album ever made. I even (and this frightens even my dykiest friends) know all the words and accompanying hand motions to "Filling Up and Spilling Over." I do not understand why John F. Kennedy Jr. is a sex symbol. I think Ann Richards should be pope.

Sitting at Henrietta Hudson's and looking at all of their expectant faces peering at me over mugs of Guinness, I was torn. I wanted very much to spend what amounts to the equivalent of Queer Christmas with my chosen family. But I still hadn't quite gotten rid of the bad aftertaste left by the miserable experience of the year before. Besides, I am also painfully aware that, compared with the number of men's spaces, there are very few places where women can go to be alone with other women. Reading *Our Bodies, Ourselves* in college will do that to a man.

But they worked on me the rest of the afternoon, and after three or four pints and an endless stream of pleading on their part, I found myself standing in Judith's Room in line to buy a ticket. I was, of course, the only man there, and I was convinced that everyone was looking at me with grim thoughts in their hearts. I sang along with the Ferron tape that was playing, just to let them know I was harmless. I heard whispering behind me. I sang louder and leafed through a copy of *Radical Chick,* hoping the newsprint wouldn't come off on my sweaty palms.

After what seemed like days, I finally made it to the counter and asked for a ticket. The woman, who sported a THELMA & LOUISE FOR PRESIDENT T-shirt, glanced at me, then looked back again. "Is this for you?" she demanded. Eyeing the wicked-looking labrys around her neck, I briefly considered lying and telling her it was for my friend whose double shift at the co-op/women's shelter prevented her from being there herself.

"Yes?" I finally said doubtfully, fully expecting her to send me packing.

To my surprise, she actually smiled. "Good," she said emphatically, handing me a ticket. "See you there."

Relieved to have passed the first test, I went home and got ready. As the time for the dance approached, I began to have second thoughts about the whole thing. The more I thought about it, the more it seemed what Pooh would call a Very Bad Idea. I called my friends several times, trying to get out of it with a variety of excuses.

"Look," Anne said firmly. "I know for a fact that you do not have to go to a twelve-step meeting for co-dependent pet owners tonight. Blaine is in that group, and she's all distraught because it was canceled for Pride. Apparently Gertrude and Simone have hidden under the bed and refuse to come out, even for liver snaps."

"Oh, please," said Katherine. "They are not going to make you recite Dorothy Allison poetry as proof of sisterhood. Besides, you know it all anyway. I saw that autographed copy on your shelf."

"You are not coming down with a temperature," said Emma, sighing. "Now get dressed and get your ass over there. We'll meet you at 9."

Finally, they all stopped answering their phones.

Knowing that what awaited me if I didn't show up was infinitely worse than anything that could happen at the dance, I dutifully walked over to the college where it was being held. Especially for the occasion I wore a T-shirt I had found that read LESBIAN TRAPPED IN A MAN'S BODY. It had seemed fun and carefree when I'd purchased it, but now I felt as though I was just asking for trouble. When I arrived at the school, I began to panic in earnest. There were about 2,000 women thronging the walkway. And me. I tried to be inconspicuous. But nothing could change the fact that I stand six foot two in my boots and am quite a bit hairier than most women. In short, I did not blend.

I half expected the women at the door to send me right home. But they took my ticket, stamped my hand, and let me in. I vaguely wondered if I had been given a blue ink stamp on purpose but decided not to worry about it. Even if I'd wanted to, there was no turning back against the incoming tide of bodies anyway. Once inside, my anxiety grew when I couldn't immediately find my friends and thought they'd abandoned me to a horrible fate. But after a few minutes of frantic searching, I discovered that they had very kindly situated themselves at the back of the room, forcing me to wade through swarms of dancing women to get to them. They thought it was funny.

"See any hot prospects?" one of them asked evilly.

"Just one," I shot back. "But it turns out she only likes butches."

We talked for a while, then hit the dance floor. I was so preoccupied with trying not to knock over anyone smaller than myself that I forgot about my shirt. Then just as I was finally relaxing, I noticed a woman pointing at me and laughing.

That's it, I thought. *They've figured it out, and they're going to make an example of me.*

The pointer worked her way over to me. In her fifties, she had a crew cut and wore a leather jacket with a skull painted on it. She reminded me of all the old-guard dykes I saw playing pool at the bar near my apartment, the kind who spoke fondly of the days when femmes were femmes. The Grim Reaper had come for me, and she was one butch number.

She stopped in front of me and looked me up and down, as though confirming that she would have no problem taking me down. I glanced around and saw that all of my friends had backed away. So much for family.

"I just want you to know," the Reaper said in a gravelly voice, "that I'm glad you're here. Thanks for coming — it means a lot." She gripped my hand in a viselike shake. Then she kissed me and disappeared back into the crowd.

I stood there for a minute, stunned, not knowing what to think. I wasn't sure if I was more surprised that I was still alive or that I'd just been kissed by a woman more masculine than any of my dates had ever been. Now that the tension I had been feeling was broken, I started to look around me. On the dance floor were women of all shapes, colors, and sizes. Their ages ranged from young teens to women well into their golden years. Women in Chanel suits danced alongside women in combat boots and flannel. I noticed five or six women in wheelchairs.

In some ways it was a complete parody of every lesbian stereotype. But it was also very real, and it suddenly occurred to me why everything felt different. It wasn't just that I was the only man around. I had attended dances before, but they had all been sponsored by and for men. At those dances, the groups were hardly what could be called mixed. The less-than-beautiful never belonged. Likewise the old, the disabled, women, or, for the most part, minorities. Sometimes someone from another group would manage to sneak in, but he usually spent his evening alone and ignored.

During the course of the evening, over a hundred women (I stopped counting at 136) came up and said something to me about my shirt. Countless others smiled or laughed without saying a word. It got to the point where I suddenly noticed my friends were being suspiciously silent.

"What's wrong?" I asked Anne, who was leaning against the wall sullenly.

She gave me a black look. "You're talking to more women than we are!" she wailed.

"Yeah," said Katherine. "I thought that cute woman in the leather mini and the Wonderbra was coming over to flirt with me, but all she wanted to do was hug *you*."

At one point someone grabbed my arm. "Hey," she demanded loudly, "are you a real girl?"

For a brief, horrible moment I was transported back to that first horrible pier dance, when my friend had been asked that same question. Only this time the question was meant in fun, posed by someone with no malice in her voice. Instead of questioning my right to be there, she asked me to slow dance. She led.

I suppose there were some women at the dance that night who objected to my being there. But if there were, they were kind enough not to let me know. Unlike other "community" events I have been to, the criteria for belonging were not physical beauty, political correctness, or a well-honed ability to make other people feel less than acceptable. Rather, the people at this dance were all there because we wanted to celebrate together what we spend so much of our time fighting for — the ability to be lesbian and gay people without having to live up to other people's standards.

Camille Paglia says that the lesbian and gay community will not advance until we learn to stop thinking in terms of gay and straight. I would add that we also must stop thinking in terms of women and men and start thinking in terms of people. We have enough other battles to fight with outside enemies; it's time to end the ones within our own family.

In the past I've noticed the relative invisibility of women at a lot of community events I have attended. But I never really thought about why it is that lesbians and gay men do so few things together. Now I know. Just like in junior high, when they suddenly grew six inches and developed breasts way before we needed to shave or wear jockstraps, the girls are still waiting for the boys to catch up.

I'm Not Saying
It's Wrong...

A few weeks ago, while vigorously avoiding doing any actual work, I flipped to C-SPAN. I like checking in with C-SPAN periodically because during the day they are prone to televising United States governmental hearings. The government, not surprisingly, is very fond of holding meetings. It has, in fact, perfected it to an art form, so that watching one of the hearings is much like watching a performance of *The Nutcracker* or *Aida* but without the dancing and singing or fun costumes. Fortunately for those of us who like this sort of thing, the government holds meetings about practically everything, from who's really to blame for the state of welfare to who's really to blame for the state of West Virginia. Twelve hours of watching reveals that no one wants to claim any knowledge of either one, but seeing democracy in action is a wonderful thing.

When I flipped to the channel, they were airing a congressional committee hearing about gay marriage. These are the best kinds of meetings to catch, because unlike standard procedural proceedings, they are controversial and involve far more yelling and tension than, say, deciding whether to add an amendment to Sen. Kennedy's harbor clean-up bill that says no Republicans have to give up their golfing allowances. It's sort of like

184

the difference between a Rangers-Bruins face-off in the Stanley Cup finals and a predinner game of street hockey featuring the neighborhood kids. Both may have the same basic goal, but one is sure to be bloodier.

Now, to fully appreciate the enormous scope of this event, one must know that whenever some major subject is up for debate, Congress decides to hold a party. To this party they invite many people who are rumored to have interesting ideas about the subject at hand. This is all done in the name of making everyone informed, so that solid decisions about crucial issues can be made after hearing the facts from all the different angles.

What they don't tell you is that everyone invited to the party has already been screened, so that the panelists know exactly what they're going to say. They also don't tell you that normal people are never invited. You have to have written a book (not necessarily on the actual subject being discussed), taught a class at a prestigious university (again, subject matter is irrelevant), or once spoken to someone who did either of these things. If I were an unkind sort, I might even suggest that certain people are picked precisely because of what they're going to say on national television when cued by their respective sponsors. But we all know that doesn't happen in America, where we are fair to everyone, even when we don't agree with them.

All in all, these panels tend to be quite agreeable, especially if one watches them instead of writing the book one has promised one's editor will be finished and on her desk the next day. It was with this spirit that I watched part of the hearings. As I said, the subject was gay marriage. Specifically, as near as I could tell, the whole point of this hearing was to educate various government types about why gay people should or should not be allowed to marry, which of course is suddenly of utmost importance since all the fuss in Hawaii began. This is so that when the time comes for elected officials to decide whether they should support such legislation, these newly educated souls can claim to have done their research and then guiltlessly vote exactly the way they would have if they hadn't wasted six hours and millions of dollars on the hearings.

For this event, four people had been invited to share their views with the esteemed panel of congresspeople — two of them pro–gay marriage and two of them con. I have forgotten most of them, but they were all, I'm sure, very informed and very interesting, mainly because none of them was Ariana Huffington. I couldn't really tell, though, because I was having a hard time figuring out which ones supported and which ones did not support gay marriage. This is another fascinating aspect of con-gressional committee meetings: No one really knows who's on whose side, because everyone is from Harvard and uses enormously long words. By the time you've looked them up, they've moved on to someone else, because the speakers get only five minutes, and they're racing the clock. The representatives attending the meet-ings have large staffs of well-educated young people who flock about them like pigeons, whispering in their ears and translating what's being said by the speakers, so that their bosses know whether to smile or frown. Those of us at home have no such luxury and must muddle through as best we can.

The fourth person I do remember, however, because he did not use any long words. His name, as I recall, was Dennis Prager. From what I understand, Mr. Prager is the host of a popular radio talk show in California. My apologies to him for not knowing his work. I'm sure he is as unaware of me as I am of him, which I think makes us even. I'm sure he's very nice, though. He looked kind of like a big Phil Donahue, without the suspenders or Marlo Thomas.

Of all the panelists, Mr. Prager was the only one I thought truly deserved to be given air time. Now, just so you save a lot of time wondering, Mr. Prager is one of the people who does not like gay marriage. This, of course, makes him a little less nice than he might be. But I still found him fascinating, for unlike some of the other speakers, who didn't like gay marriage because it was "icky" and "wrong," Mr. Prager has a theory, which he stands behind 100 percent. According to Mr. Prager, his theory is based entirely on science. You can't argue with that.

Mr. Prager's theory is that everyone — himself included — is inherently bisexual. This, he says, is the fundamental nature of humankind. How we choose to act on this nature, however, is what concerns him. See, he thinks that expressing the homosexual aspect of sexuality is immoral. Why? Because the Judeo-Christian tradition (this is the new term for *Bible,* by the way) that we have adopted as our fundamental way of life in America says so. It also says that we should all get married as soon as possible and begin popping out Judeo-Christian children.

This is where the gay marriage part comes in and it all gets really good. What Mr. Prager believes is the correct thing to do is to suppress the homosexual aspects of our sexualities and allow the heterosexual aspects to flourish. According to his thinking, allowing gay people to marry will send a message to young people that being gay is acceptable. Discovering that this is now an option to them, they would then cease to repress their homosexual sides and become born-again dykes and fags. He also fears that people who have already properly suppressed their homosexual sides and married will suddenly feel they have been given permission to abandon spouses and families to attend the Michigan Womyn's Music Festival and purchase condos in South Beach.

It is far better, he feels, to make homosexuality seem forbidden, so that no one will want to do it in the first place. This wonderful theory is based, according to Mr. Prager, on interviews he has conducted with "leading sex researchers." And he apparently knows a lot of them. Why they weren't invited to speak about their own views is something we did not have time to get into. Perhaps there was not enough room in the rotunda to hold them all.

Mr. Prager says he has no problem with gay people, which relieved those of us who were beginning to worry. Barney Frank, the openly gay representative from Massachusetts, asked Mr. Prager if he had a problem with Frank and his lover speaking to teenagers about being gay. Mr. Prager said he did not, because being gay is still seen as something freakish, and no self-respecting teenager would want to be freakish. Mr. Prager has apparently missed the proliferation of nose rings and tribal body art in the twelve-year-old set, or perhaps he is simply acquainted with a better class of young people than am I. At any rate he did not, he continued, think "legitimizing" Frank's relationship by allowing him to marry was a good idea, because then it would make kids want to be gay too. A more rational approach, he feels, is to create a society in which repressing homosexual feelings is considered a positive thing. I briefly wondered if he'd ever visited a single-sex junior high school during gym class.

Now, here's why Mr. Prager impressed me. With his simple statement, he launched a brilliant new campaign by the right wing. First, he admitted that homosexual tendencies are perfectly normal — we all have them. In this way he removed himself from the ultraconservative stance favored by people like Jesse Helms, whose supporters are easy to ridicule or to label hatemongers because they attempt to separate queers from everyone else as being somehow tainted. By becoming one of "us," at least theoretically, Prager became part of the family, albeit it a distant cousin.

Second, he then went on to say that, although these desires may be normal, ultimately any expression of them is harmful to society, which benefits from the coupling of two sexes together to form family units. Thus he brought back into his camp any of the anti–gay marriage people he might have lost with his earlier admission of homo leanings. Who isn't for anything pro-family?

In short, Mr. Prager admitted that although he might have inclinations to act a certain way, by using discretion and clearheaded thinking about what was best for everyone, he did not do so. This, by inference, makes him (and everyone like him who would love to suck cock or munch muff but is too afraid to and so doesn't) better people. They aren't hateful, or bigoted, or mean. They're patriotic. They are good citizens because they have sacrificed something that might have made them happy for the more important good of their neighbors, their children, their country. Homosexuals, in comparison, are not precisely wicked, just weak-willed, like people who gleefully inhale nicotine even though it's known to kill, in the process poisoning everyone around them with second-hand smoke just so they can fulfill their personal addiction. Apparently, those of us who "actively practice" homosexuality are guilty of throwing off second-hand queerness.

This is an absolutely flawless campaign. By admitting that you have the inclination to do something — say, commit murder — but then denying that you did it because it "just wouldn't be right," you allow yourself to be seen as someone who has clearly weighed all the options and chosen that which will benefit the most people. This allows others who might have previously felt guilty about having those same inclinations themselves to warm to you. "Of course I thought about murdering my wife. I even talked about it. But I could never actually do it." What a nice man. Of course we've all thought those things. Thank you for making us feel normal. Go home to Brentwood.

Now, no one was comparing being queer to murder, but you get the idea. If you buy Mr. Prager's arguments, everybody wins. Homophobes can feel better about themselves, because having queer thoughts is okay so long as you don't do anything about it. And actually being queer can reclaim some of the decadence it seems to have lost over the past decade or so. Instead of being freaks, we can see ourselves as flouting morals we simply don't agree with. Like the draft dodgers of old, we can rush up to Canada until the homophobes find something else to whine about. Chelsea Clinton, having followed in her father's footsteps, pardons us all and we're finally, if reluctantly, seen as the true rebels we always were, fighting for a just cause.

Or maybe not. Outwardly, Mr. Prager's five-minute speech was idiocy at its best. Kids won't want to do something because it's forbidden? We should all marry and pop out babies because it's what we've agreed to do as a society? Nonsense. This is pure right-wing conservatism masquerading as social conscience, and it's great fun to laugh at.

But therein lies the danger. People love idiots who seem like patriots, because they make the rest of us look good. I need only to point to the twelve years of presidents Reagan and Bush as proof. People like men with easy answers who make them feel good for having no idea what they really think. If Mr. Prager's way of thinking were to spread, queers would be seen as people who simply aren't willing to do enough for their country, while nonqueer people (in Mr. Prager's world no one is exactly straight) are simply doing what's right for everyone. It's the classic parental guilt statement: "I'm not saying what you did was wrong; I just said I was disappointed."

And Mr. Prager is disappointed. We in the queer community have failed him utterly. And if legal gay marriage becomes a reality in this country, we will have also failed both the suddenly unrepressed lesbians and gay men who will leave their hitherto happy families, as well as the many innocent children who will see us as people to emulate and who will undoubtedly trip merrily down the garden path in reckless defiance of Mr. Prager's Judeo-Christian vision of America. If he and his followers have their way, perhaps one day we'll wake up to find the streets plastered with posters like the ones minted during World War II urging Americans to be on the lookout for possible Nazis in their midst. A grim-faced Big Brother will be pointing a wary finger at two men or two women holding hands, while beneath his watchful gaze the words IT'S YOUR DUTY will appear in hellish red.

A Slightly Dented Childhood

If Jesus Loves Me, Why Hasn't He Called?

For many children in America, Sunday is a day of rest. It might involve a quick trip to Mass, or possibly a boring yet harmless trip to Grandma's for some pot roast and cheek pinching, but in general it is a day of sleeping in, of long hours spent doing nothing, of going to the beach or to the park for fun-filled picnics. Not for me. As a child, my Sundays were spent in Baptist Concentration Camp, a hideous den of horrors cleverly disguised with the innocent moniker Sunday School.

On the surface it all seemed harmless enough. Each Sunday morning, while our parents congregated in the sanctuary above us, fifteen or twenty freshly scrubbed youngsters would crowd into the Immanuel Baptist Church's gold-carpeted basement, where we would seat ourselves quietly on folding chairs and wait expectantly for the weekly ritual to begin. At precisely 9 o'clock, Mrs. Evans would come in, her polyester dress bouncing merrily about her large breasts and ample behind. Mrs. Evans was the commandant of Sunday School, and she took it very seriously. Childless herself due to an ovarian cyst (I heard my mother talking about it once), she had dedicated her life to nurturing the immortal souls of the young.

She took to it with unmatched fervor and over the years had honed her weekly routine into a spiritual workout guaranteed to make us tireless laborers for Jesus.

First came prayer. At Mrs. Evans's command, we stood and attempted to maintain our balance with our eyes closed while she recited the litany of things for which we should be thankful (our families, church, food, government) and things we should be concerned about (poor people, hungry people, people without governments, people who didn't have Sunday School). If there was something particular to the church family that needed attention, such as a sick child, a dying elder, or a new roof fund, that would get thrown in at the end. It all ended with a group "Amen!" said enthusiastically in the way that is bred into all Baptist children.

After the praying came the Sword Drill. According to Mrs. Evans, our greatest enemy in life was Satan. She never really explained exactly who he was, but we were led to believe that he was most definitely not someone who had attended Sunday School as a child and was therefore bad news. As such, we were instructed that we must be on constant guard for his tempting ways, although, again, what these ways were was never quite spelled out, leaving most of us with the firm impression that Satan was a cross between a used-car salesman and Farrah Fawcett, who in the 1970s was considered something of a tramp by good Baptist people.

Our weapon against Satan, explained Mrs. Evans, was the Bible, which we should always think of as a sword with which to slay him, should the need arise. Somehow this didn't seem as effective to me as a smart handgun would have, but Mrs. Evans was older and therefore knew better. The purpose of the Sword Drill was, essentially, to practice killing Satan. Holding our Bibles/swords at our sides, we would wait until Mrs. Evans called out a particular verse. Then we would draw our swords and flip frantically through the pages looking for the reference she'd given. Whoever found it first would begin to read it in a loud voice, thus scoring a direct hit on the Evil One. The rest of us, apparently, became casualties of friendly fire.

The Sword Drill lasted through five or six verses, until Mrs. Evans was assured that at least some of us had correctly memorized the order of the books of the Bible, or at least had the presence of mind to install clever little tabs with the names of the books printed on them, effectively creating the biblical equivalent of a semiautomatic weapon. Should we be particularly slow to use our swords, Mrs. Evans would shriek in a frantic voice, "Satan is getting closer! Satan is winning! Do you want Satan to beat you?" sending us into a panic as we scrambled for our ammunition.

Military maneuvers completed, it was then time for Flannelgraph. This seems to be an invention wholly original to Baptist Sunday School classrooms, which is really a pity, because in the right hands it could actually be quite fun. The Flannelgraph is a large board covered in black felt. Placed upon the board are paper dolls that have been backed with a flocked material that makes them stick to the felt. Using the paper dolls, a clever person can re-create an infinite variety of scenes. Handy books are provided filled with cut-out Jesuses, apostles, trees, farm animals, boats, food, demon-possessed vagrants, and anything else one might need for hours of Flannelgraph enjoyment. Like I said, it could be fun. But as with so many things, the Christian element makes it not as cheery as it might otherwise be, limiting it as it does to the retelling of Bible stories.

Mrs. Evans' favorite story in the Bible was, of course, the Crucifixion and Resurrection of Jesus Christ. She had told the story so often that she was able to maneuver the Flannelgraph figures about the board in such a way as to hold us captivated while she described the judgment, torture, and execution of our Lord.

Up went the Pontius Pilate paper doll, scorning the Jesus doll. "And they whipped him!" Mrs. Evans screeched, her meaty hands flailing in imitation of the lashes as she moved the paper Roman guard toward Jesus.

Then away they went, only to be replaced by Jesus, wearing a crown of thorns and carrying his paper cross on wounded shoulders while a paper crowd jeered cruelly, Mrs. Evans providing all of the taunting voices. Once at Calvary, up went Jesus and his cross, along with the two thieves crucified with him. A weeping paper Mary and the apostles brave enough to attend sat at the base.

"He hung there for three days!" Mrs. Evans said, her voice rising. "Three days! And on the third day, he died!" She let the last word hang in the air as we stared, wide-eyed, at the Flannelgraph. It was all very vivid, and by the time she rolled the paper stone away from the paper grave, we were beside ourselves.

There were, of course, other stories. And Mrs. Evans knew them all by heart. There was a paper Daniel in the lions' den, and Jesus walking on a paper sea. There were paper angels and paper clouds, and even a paper heaven with streets of gold. It was all glorious. Yet we were forbidden to actually touch the Flannelgraph materials ourselves.

Once, though, we did touch them. Mrs. Evans was out of the room, and the Flannelgraph was left unguarded. Scottie Hogan, who I can now only assume was under the influence of Satan, ran up and snatched a paper apostle Paul from the box. He then proceeded to reenact a scene from *Saturday Night Fever,* with Paul assuming the John Travolta role. The rest of us went wild, grabbing assorted figures and making them boogie-oogie-oogie along with Paul/John on the Flannelgraph disco floor. Somehow, we managed to put everything back in the box before Mrs. Evans returned, and if she ever wondered why we all were looking guiltily at our feet when she entered the room, she didn't let on.

The next item on the weekly agenda was arts and crafts. This gave us time to recover from the overwhelming influence of the Flannelgraph. Seated around conveniently child-sized tables, we would be instructed in any manner of Christian handiwork, all designed to further our love for Jesus and deepen our commitment to his work. A typical project would involve re-creating a biblical event (such as Noah's ark or the feeding of the 5,000) in Play-Doh or finger paints. Holiday-themed crafts were especially nice, as they generally involved the use of cotton balls, glue, glitter, and other exciting items that left us giddy with the creative spirit. On one memorable occasion, we cut Jesus's face out of a picture and decoupaged it onto Ivory soap, ensuring that every time we washed our hands we would be reminded of his cleansing love. My mother kept my soap in the guest bathroom, where for three years startled visitors left it untouched.

Lest things become too cheerful and lighthearted, crafts was followed by the weekly Missionary Report. Our class had "adopted" a missionary family. They lived somewhere in Africa, where we were told they were saving the souls of the heathens, who we saw selfishly preferred tending their crops and worshiping ancestral deities to holding Sword Drills and Flannelgraph. Slowly, however, our missionary family was making inroads. We knew this because they wrote us letters telling us how many souls they had saved each month. We had a map of their country, and for every ten souls, Mrs. Evans placed another big gold star on the map.

Our job was to send money to the family. We had each been given a bank in the shape of a globe. Each week we were supposed to put as much money as we could into the bank, then bring it to Sunday School. There, at the appointed time, we would march to the front of the room and empty our bank's contents into a big bowl under the watchful eye of Mrs. Evans. If our contribution was large, we were awarded with a beaming smile and a card imprinted with an encouraging Bible verse about people who supported missionaries getting wonderful rewards in heaven.

If, however, our weekly earnings fell below an acceptable level, we were told to stand before the class and inform everyone what we had bought that week with money that clearly could have been better used. After one or two Sundays of having to look into the disappointed faces of your classmates and admit that you had purchased one too many packages of gum or yet another *Star Wars* action figure, the lesson was learned: Our sin was causing the Lord's work to suffer.

My favorite part of Sunday School was the song period, simply because it was an excuse to stand up and dance around a little bit, which normally Baptists do not do. Certainly I didn't care for the music, finding it vulgar and lacking in style. I don't know who wrote these songs, but in talking to other SS survivors, I have discovered that they are universally known. I can only suspect, then, that somewhere a secret agency is cranking out songbooks of unspeakable evil and whisking them off to churches around the world.

While most of the songs were generally cheerful and uplifting, if horribly awful, some were just plain bizarre. The worst of the lot was a song that cleverly combined knowledge of the alphabet with biblical tidbits. "A, B, C, D, E, F, G, Jesus died for you and me" went the first sing-song verse. "H, I, J, K, L, M, N, Jesus died for sinful men. Amen! O, P, Q, R, S, T, U, I believe God's word is true. U, V, W, God has promised you, X, Y, Z, a home eternally." At the time, I sang the song loudly and forcefully, proud to display my recently acquired alphabetical knowledge. Listening to it now, I get chills.

Singing marked the end of the Sunday School work-out. But on the first Sunday of each month, before sending us on our way, Mrs. Evans allowed us to partake of a junior version of the communion our parents and older siblings were receiving upstairs. Filing one by one to the front, we were presented with a Nilla Wafer and a small cup of Kool-Aid. The body and blood of Jesus Christ they weren't, but somehow we felt very grown-up and serious as we dutifully ate and drank, dreaming of the days when our cookies and fruit punch would be replaced by broken bits of cracker and grape juice doled out by the grim-faced deacons in their dark suits and greased-back hair.

Communion or not, each Sunday inevitably ended with a group sing-along of the old standby "Jesus Loves Me." Joining hands, we would sway from side to side, much like the joyous Hoos warbling away in *How the Grinch Stole Christmas*. Tiny voices raised in unison, we joined one another in the familiar words. "Yes, Jesus loves me!" we shouted. "Yes, Jesus loves me." We were one in our love for the savior and all he offered, and when it was over, we felt very good indeed.

Everything about Sunday School seemed fine for a while. In fact, for some time I felt very holy as I exited the church each Sunday, content in the knowledge that I had spent time with Jesus and done my Christian duty for yet another week. It felt good to be so much better than all of those African natives the missionaries were frantically trying to convert from their sinful ways.

Then one day, while sitting in the back seat on the ride home, things began to change. Maybe the sugar from the Nilla Wafer was too much, or maybe the heat in the basement had gone to my head. Maybe it was just that I was getting older and was starting to understand a few things I hadn't before. Whatever it was, the spell woven by Mrs. Evans, Flannelgraph, and the Kool-Aid wore off. Suddenly, my Sears three-piece suit seemed a little too warm, the clip-on tie a tad snug around my little throat. I was no longer the placid Christian child who had drawn his sword in victory. I looked down at the cross I'd made from popsicle sticks, and I started to wonder — what did it all mean?

The next week, right after Sword Drill, I raised my hand. When Mrs. Evans acknowledged me, I stood up. "I was just wondering," I said, "if Jesus loves me so much, how come he never calls or anything? My grandma loves me, and she calls every Tuesday night to tell me so."

Mrs. Evans's smile froze. She stared at me. Then she took a deep breath. "Well, Michael," she said, "Jesus isn't really a person like you are or like your grandmother is. He can't just pick up the phone and call. He talks to us in other ways."

There was rustling around me. This was the first any of us had ever heard about Jesus not being a person like we were. "What do you mean he isn't like us?" asked Janice Preston.

Mrs. Evans didn't look happy. "Jesus is God's son," she said. "He lives up in heaven."

"Why doesn't he come down here?" I asked. The others nodded.

Mrs. Evans sighed. "He is coming down," she said. "But not yet. It isn't time yet."

"When will it be time?" I asked.

"I don't know." The smile had left Mrs. Evans's face.

"Then how do you know he's there?" I pressed. "If he doesn't talk to you."

"I just do," Mrs. Evans hissed through clenched teeth. "Because the Bible says so."

We had her, and we knew it. Every child in that room had been given the "because I said so" answer, and we all knew what it meant: She didn't really have any answers. We moved in for the kill, and we were merciless.

"Who told the people who wrote the Bible what to say?" asked Janice.

"How do you know Jesus loves us?" queried Scottie.

"If Jesus can do anything, why can't he talk to us?" I tried again.

It was a mass epiphany, and I was the leader. It was as though, as one, we had broken free from the mindless obedience that had been drummed into our heads by group sing-alongs and Sword Drills. For the first time, we were thinking on our own, and we wanted answers. No longer willing to believe everything we were told, even if it was accompanied by Flannelgraph, we wanted proof. We were filled with the fire of emancipation, and we went wild.

"If you sin while you're falling out of a tree and you die when you hit the ground, will you still go to heaven?" John Carver asked.

"Why does God make the Africans go to hell if they've never heard of him?" wondered a boy who had never spoken a word as long as I'd been in Sunday School.

"How did Mary get pregnant if she wasn't married?" I asked. It was something that had bothered me for a long time, but I'd always been afraid to ask.

By the end of the hour, Mrs. Evans was near tears. Try as she might, she couldn't get us to stop our questioning. Flannelgraph didn't work. Arts and crafts were useless. We wanted nothing of singing. We all wanted to know just why it was that Jesus had never spoken to a single person in the room. When our parents finally came to retrieve us, Mrs. Evans pushed us into their arms and fled, crying, from the room.

"What was that all about?" my mother asked, helping me on with my coat.

I fixed her with a steely-eyed stare. "If Jesus loves me," I asked, settling in for a fight, "why hasn't he called?"

When I saw her face drain of color, I knew it was going to be a long ride home.

Confessions
of a Don't-Bee

As a preschooler, one of my great joys was sitting in my parents' big bed each morning and watching *Romper Room*. For those poor souls unacquainted with the joys of this now-defunct '70s-era children's television show, I will explain. Romper Room was an idyllic day-care center, where an audience of fifteen or so lucky four- and five-year-olds sang, danced, and experienced sheer joy in the company of the world's perkiest host, Miss Nancy. I understand that different cities had different hosts, but they all uncannily seemed to resemble Miss Nancy, as though some kind of government experiment in genetic cloning had gone horribly awry, resulting in an army of identical children's television personalities with permanent smiles and poor wardrobes. A sort of Kathie Lee for the preschool set, Miss Nancy doled out love to her assembled guests while the rest of us sat at home and watched, wondering what it was we had done so as not to be allowed to join the rabidly merry kids basking in her glow.

The premise of *Romper Room* was simple indeed. Miss Nancy sang and danced. We watched. In a time when, at least in my neighborhood, many mothers remained at home with their preschool children, it provided an hour of relief for parents who simply wanted to sit and drink their coffee in peace and quiet. Entranced by the fun taking place in Miss Nancy's room, those of us still young enough to find such things thrilling would stop everything to see what new song Miss Nancy would teach us today.

At some point in every *Romper Room* show, Miss Nancy would hold up her Magic Mirror. This clever prop was simply a hand mirror with the glass removed so that Miss Nancy's buoyant face could peer through. She would stare directly at the camera through the hole in the mirror and pretend to see all of the Friends at Home while she chattered on endlessly about all the fun she and her guests were having. This was supposed to make those of us alone in our rooms feel better about not being able to romp with the more fortunate children.

As much as I loved her, I thought Miss Nancy was full of crap when it came to the Magic Mirror. Even with my rudimentary knowledge of science, I knew she couldn't really see me at home, and I considered myself much more sophisticated than the obviously demented children in the *Romper Room* studio audience who shrieked with glee whenever Miss Nancy peered at them through the Magic Mirror and pretended to be looking across the airwaves. "I see Kathy," she'd say, and Kathy would squeal and clap her hands, in awe of Miss Nancy's mystical powers. Holding Kathy in contempt, I would sit in bed with arms folded, waiting for Miss Nancy to put down the Magic Mirror and move on to something more exciting, like a rousing group-sing of "Row, Row, Row Your Boat."

This all changed, however, the day Miss Nancy was discussing the crucial issue of color. I had always been fond of color and was pleased that I was going to learn something useful that I could share later on with my parents and friends. I watched carefully as Miss Nancy held up circles of various colors and told us what they were and how they could be put together to form new colors. This impressed me greatly. After going over the relative merits of red, blue, and green, she asked the children in her studio audience what their favorite colors were. "Blue!" they shouted, or "Yellow!"

Then Miss Nancy picked up the Magic Mirror and held it in front of her face. "And what's your favorite color, Friends at Home?" she asked cheerfully.

"Purple!" I screamed back. I knew that, in the greater scheme of things, purple was a sissy color, but what did I care? I was full of Froot Loops and feeling fine. Purple was bold. It was different. And besides, Miss Nancy couldn't hear me anyway. "Purple!" I screamed again, giggling madly.

Suddenly, Miss Nancy's face inside the mirror broke into a wide smile. "I heard a Friend at Home say purple!" she chirped. "That's an *interesting* color to pick, isn't it boys and girls?"

In that instant, my safe childhood world shattered forever. Miss Nancy could hear me. Not only that but she had announced to the world that a Friend at Home actually preferred purple over blue or yellow. I stared at the television in horror, waiting for all the children in the *Romper Room* world to turn on me and begin laughing derisively.

Then, just as the enormity of what had happened began to sink in, another terrible thought entered my four-year-old brain. If Miss Nancy could hear me, then surely she could see me as well. Apparently, my knowl-

edge of how television worked was flawed in a fundamental way, resulting in my horrible admission of being
a boy who loved a color I thought only little girls were
supposed to favor. Who knew what else Miss Nancy
knew about me. She might have seen me engaging in my
favorite hobby of thumb sucking. Worse, she might actually be aware that on occasion I not only picked my nose
but actually ate what came out.

Unable to think clearly, I did what any reasonable
child would do: I hid under the bed. There, secure among
the dust bunnies, I peered out at Miss Nancy, watching
anxiously as she put down the Magic Mirror and moved
on to the next activity. I breathed a sigh of relief, thinking that maybe she had forgotten about me. The calm was
short-lived, however, when there was a knock on the
Romper Room door and Miss Nancy went to answer it.
Throwing wide the door, she turned to the camera and
beamed. "Hey, everyone, it's Do-Bee!" she cried.

Do-Bee was the *Romper Room* mascot and was, in
fact, a gigantic yellow and black bee, complete with
wings and bouncing antennae. Once every day, Do-Bee
would come into the room and greet all of the children.
He would buzz around, and the kids would go mad,
jumping up and down and pawing at Do-Bee's clever
costume. Invariably, Do-Bee would cover his mouth with
his hands and appear to giggle. Much later, I would realize that Do-Bee was, all along, a Queen Bee. At the time
I simply thought he was fabulous.

The purpose of Do-Bee was to teach us all the
things we should do or be. "We all want to be good Do-
Bees, don't we, boys and girls?" Miss Nancy would say
after a lesson on sharing or the importance of neatness,
and we would all nod agreeably. The opposite of a Do-

Bee was, of course, a Don't-Bee, a title no self-respecting child would claim. Satisfied that we were all normal and properly oriented, Do-Bee would then depart, antennae bouncing merrily, to pollinate the flowers or make honey or whatever he did in his off hours.

Normally, I welcomed the appearance of Do-Bee. I enjoyed his cheerful way of dancing from foot to foot and waving at the camera. But now everything had changed. If Miss Nancy could see me, so, of course, could Do-Bee. Suddenly, in a moment of sheer horror, it all came together in my mind. Do-Bee was Miss Nancy's hench-man, the bee who carried out her dirty work. His brief appearance each day gave her the opportunity to point out the Friends at Home whose bad behavior she'd spied in the Magic Mirror. Thus identified as Don't-Bees, those children were then the targets of Do-Bee's wrath.

Clearly, after my declaration of purple-loving, I was now a Don't-Bee.

I scurried out from under the bed and turned off the television, severing the channel between me and Miss Nancy. But I feared it was too late. For the rest of the day, I walked around in terror, waiting for Do-Bee to come for me. I imagined him taking me away to wherever it was that children who didn't like normal colors like blue and yellow were kept. I pictured rows of cages holding children who, like me, had innocently admitted some ter-rible transgression. Perhaps they'd refused to smile at one of Miss Nancy's little jokes or been unable to keep up in Duck, Duck Goose. Maybe they'd sat sullenly while everyone else jumped rope, or, heaven forbid, colored outside the lines. Then, as they went about their days, they were suddenly plucked from their homes by Do-Bee and whisked away.

And if Miss Nancy was capable of such treachery, my feverish mind said, surely Captain Kangaroo was in on it as well. I thought of all the times I'd laughed innocently at Mr. Greenjeans's jokes, while in all likelihood he was watching my every move and taking notes, and I was filled with terror. By the end of the day, I'd developed a complete conspiracy theory that I was certain involved the core players of all major children's television programs. After gathering their information, Miss Nancy and the Captain would meet with Mr. Rogers, and possibly Bozo, at their secret headquarters. Together they would draw up a list of children who, for one reason or another, just did not fit in. Then, that night, Do-Bee would sweep through their homes like an angel of death, gathering up the wayward kids and taking them, I was certain, to Mr. Rogers's Kingdom of Make-Believe, where they would be held captive in Lady Elaine's merry-go-round. Lady Elaine, with her androgynous and slightly creepy appearance, had always frightened me in a vague way. Now I knew why — she was just waiting to get her twisted little puppet hands on me.

For the next week I slept fitfully, fearful that if I dozed off I'd next wake in some dank prison surrounded by other lovers of purple. My mother wondered why I didn't clamor any longer for my morning dose of *Romper Room,* preferring instead to actually play outdoors, constantly looking over my shoulder. "Don't you want to see *The Magic Toyshop?*" she asked, shaking her head in wonder when I turned pale and retreated to my room to build yet another Lego fortress. I avoided the television studiously, certain that now even Bobby and Cindy Brady weren't to be trusted. Surely they, too, were under the control of Miss Nancy and the evil children's television cabal.

Things went on in this way for some time. At first I could hardly walk outside my bedroom without fear of being ambushed. I jumped at the slightest sound and went to pieces at the merest hint of buzzing. I even tried to ward off Do-Bee by painting lots of pictures in bright, primary colors and hanging them on my bedroom wall. Perhaps, I thought, Miss Nancy would look into her Magic Mirror and see that I had changed. I hid my purple shirt and my purple bathrobe and my purple shorts and wore only blue or green things. I was determined to be normal, even if it made me miserable.

Then one day I was sent to a friend's house to stay while my mother did errands. Andy's mother sat us in the family room and turned on the television to *Sesame Street*. For some reason I cannot now imagine, I had never seen the show before. It was, however, Andy's favorite, and he immediately became engrossed in learning about the number *9* and the letter *q*. Terrified, I hid behind a beanbag chair, waiting for the moment when yet another Big Brother figure would appear, pointing an accusing finger at the boy who admitted to a queer fondness for inappropriate shades.

When Big Bird came on, I trembled, watching his enormous, never-closing eyes for signs of spying. Even larger than Do-Bee, his huge feet and sharp beak looked capable of tearing a small boy to bits. I glanced at Andy, who was laughing at the deceptively affable bird's comic antics, and wondered if I should warn him about the danger he was exposing himself to. Doing so would be risking putting myself in further danger, especially since, like Miss Nancy, Big Bird had also said hello to the "friends at home." By now wise to the ways of the conspiracy, I knew that was a sign.

Andy was my friend, and I owed it to him to protect him from the clutches of Do-Bee and Big Bird. I had to speak out. But before I could utter a word of warning, Big Bird left and the scene switched to one featuring Bert and Ernie. Momentarily flustered by these new players in the game, I stayed in my hiding place and watched them for a minute to see what diabolical tricks they would try to use against me.

Despite my fears there was something about the on-screen pair that spoke to me, something I could relate to. Unlike the odd speechless rabbit of Captain Kangaroo, or Do-Bee's silent gesturing filled with ominous meanings, they were friendly and nonthreatening. Sure, Bert's single eyebrow was disconcerting, and he did look vaguely menacing. But Ernie's happy, smiling face reassured me. His sprightly tuft of hair made me laugh, and his gaily striped sweater looked like one I myself owned.

But more than that, there was something different about the way Bert and Ernie related to each other, something I had never seen before in all my hours of television watching. They joked amiably as they ate cookies together. They talked to each other about the things they liked. They went to sleep in their shared bedroom. They seemed to like each other in a way I could understand. On some deep level I didn't fully understand, I was certain that they too probably liked purple.

Eventually I came out from behind the beanbag chair, sat down, and watched some more. Soon I was laughing delightedly as Ernie counted sheep and Bert tossed restlessly beside him, all thoughts of Miss Nancy driven from my mind. While I wasn't entirely convinced that the menacing Do-Bee and his friends weren't still out there, waiting to pounce on children who didn't live up to their expectations, now I knew that I had friends on my side. There were others like me. Others who didn't quite fit in but who were nonetheless happy. That night, imagining Ernie asleep in a bed next to mine, I slept peacefully for the first time in days.

Packing for the Second Coming

When I was seven years old, I packed for the Second Coming of Jesus Christ, Our Savior. I did it in shoe boxes — seventeen of them — filled to near bursting with everything I thought I might need in the great hereafter. I even labeled them: PHOTOS, ART SUPPLIES, *STAR WARS* FIGURES. After watching my mother organize countless moves from house to house as our family trotted around the globe, I knew how it was done, and I was a model of efficiency. When I got to heaven, I would know exactly which box my toothbrush was in.

The hardest part was choosing which of my cherished items to leave behind. I knew from what my mother had told me about the streets being paved with gold that money was no good in heaven, so I left out my piggy bank. But being a veteran of school lunch-hour sandwich swaps, I had a vague suspicion that some form of barter was sure to exist behind the pearly gates, just as it did in the cafeteria of Westgate Elementary School. So in went the chrome-plated Collector's Series Hot Wheels cars my friend Mickey and I jealously collected. They were the rarest thing I owned, next to the shark tooth my grandmother had sent me from Florida, and I was sure they would come in handy.

Clothes were not a problem, since it had been made abundantly clear to me early on that everyone up there wore only shining gowns of whitest silk. Despite this fact, it was with some reluctance that I left my favorite item of clothing — my *Hee Haw* overalls — folded in the drawer. I assumed also that accessories would be thoughtfully provided, so I left my Captain Crunch Decoder Ring in its box, albeit wistfully. Since my mother had never been completely clear as to the status of pets in the afterlife, I threw in a stack of photos of the hamsters, the dogs, and the cat. Of these, the cat and one of the hamsters had already preceded me into the beyond, and I half believed I would find them waiting when I arrived. But being a sensible child, I figured it couldn't hurt to prepare for the worst. Photos of my family remained behind, as I innocently expected them all to be there with me.

The remainder of the boxes housed my extensive collection of *Charlie's Angels* trading cards. I couldn't really think of what I would do with them once I arrived in my lord's bosom, but I had put more effort into collecting and organizing them than I had into anything else I'd ever done in my short life, and I wasn't leaving them behind. Secretly, I hoped that one of the rewards awaiting me (and I was positive there were rewards) was the hard-to-find card featuring Kelly in hot pants that had long eluded me.

Two things were responsible for this frenzy of packing. One was the approaching American bicentennial celebration of 1976. For months I'd heard about this wondrous time, and although I had no idea what it actually was, I figured anything that could inspire both a newly minted quarter and a series of McDonald's commemorative jelly glasses must be of some significance.

The only thing I could conceive of being worthy of such honors was the return of Jesus, which both the pastor of our church and my mother insisted would happen soon but, when pressed, could not put an exact date on. Putting two and two together, I thought myself very clever indeed for unraveling the mystery that had puzzled biblical scholars for centuries.

The second, and probably most influential, thing was a charming little song called "I Wish We'd All Been Ready," which I'd recently heard one of my sisters playing on her stereo. It was sung by a Christian rock singer named Larry Norman, and it was all about the unbelievers who were left behind when Jesus came to sweep up his chosen people before the world was burned up in the end times. For whatever reason it had gained some amount of popularity among the teenage Christian set that summer and was quickly replacing Ocean's "Put Your Hand in the Hand" as the anthem of socially conscious American youth.

It says something about the nature of Norman's cheery ditty that I can still remember most of it today. It isn't hard, really, because essentially each verse was a mini-horror movie about another unfortunate soul shocked into awareness of his or her sinful existence by the sudden disappearance of a more pious friend or loved one during the rapture. Take, for instance, my personal favorite line: "A man and wife asleep in bed, she hears a noise and turns her head [dramatic pause] he's gone." Just in case the message was somehow lost, the chorus nailed it home. "I wish we'd all been ready. There's no time to change your mind; the son has come, and you've been left behind."

Children, they say, are visual creatures to begin with. In my little, and admittedly overactive, mind, I saw a woman rolling over in bed, only to find it empty because her husband (who of course had begged her for years to accept Christ in preparation for just this kind of thing) had flown up to heaven, leaving her to face the tortures of Armageddon, not to mention the bills and hungry pets, all by herself. From there it was but a small leap to picturing myself waking up one sunny morning and going in search of my family, only to find the house empty and Satan himself knocking at the front door.

I decided that the Fourth of July would be The Day. I knew that the Fourth was the special occasion everyone was waiting for, and I was certain Jesus would want to make a big entrance. It made sense (to me, anyway) that he would surprise everyone by showing up in time for the fireworks and picnics I was told were in the planning. Having determined that the time was upon us, I prepared accordingly. When I'd packed everything and sealed it tightly with tape, I arranged the boxes in a pile. Then I attended to my traveling wardrobe. According to my mother, what one wore for a trip was of utmost importance, especially if traveling long distances. I had no idea how far heaven was from Virginia, but since John Denver swore that West Virginia was "almost heaven," I assumed it was probably somewhere above Route 19, perhaps near Gaithersburg. I'd been there once, and I recalled that the ride back featured only one pit stop at Dairy Queen, which meant it wasn't too far.

Opening my closet, I thought about what outfit would be most fetching in the eyes of the Lord, Our God. While I knew that shortly after arrival I would be shedding my earthly clothes for those of heavenly design, I wanted to make a good first impression. After pausing briefly at my green polyester three-piece suit purchased especially for Easter, I decided instead on an ensemble of shorts and a shirt, which the attached raccoon Garanimal tags assured me were perfectly suited for each other in both color and form. They were lightweight — which I was certain would be an advantage when being lifted up to God — and sporty.

After dressing, I sat on my bed and waited. I wasn't entirely sure what I was waiting for, but I did it patiently and expectantly. No one had ever explained to me exactly what would happen when the rapture occurred, but I had some ideas. Drawing from a variety of sources, I had determined that there would probably not be much warning and that it would all be over rather quickly. Those who were left on Earth would suddenly discover themselves riding in cars without drivers, talking to companions who were no longer there, and becoming tangled in jump ropes as the turners on either side were whisked away to the great reward.

I confess I was secretly thrilled by the idea of unmanned cars skidding around the roads while the sinners inside screamed, and I hoped I'd get to see it. I also allowed myself to wonder, momentarily and a little guiltily, if all of my family members would really be joining me on the trip. It strikes me odd now that I didn't tell any of them of my plans. I like to think that I was just preoccupied with the preparations and that there was no malice of forethought in my secrecy.

As for myself, I suppose I expected the heavens to open up and to feel myself being raised gently into the skies like a kite, or like the revolving swing ride at the annual state fair, giving me a good view of all the doubters below crying out for forgiveness as I hovered, saved, above their heads. I wondered if it would feel like being in an airplane, which I was by then a veteran of due to many trips overseas. I hoped someone would present me with a plastic pin commemorating the event, as a friendly pilot had once done on a Pan American flight my family took from Africa back to America.

And so I sat and waited. After a few minutes, when everything seemed to be going on just as it had before I'd packed, I started to wonder if maybe something was a little off in my timing. I tried to remember whether Norman had specified precisely what time the Son was coming. I thought about going downstairs and getting my sister's record of the song and checking the liner notes for clues, but I feared that being separated from my belongings when the blessed event occurred would be a tactical error similar to attempting to check through nine pieces of luggage and two pets at Heathrow while changing planes for Venice. My father had done this once, and we'd arrived in Italy with three cats and six bags, none of which were our own, while our two Irish setters and my favorite shirt made their way to Rome. While I knew it was not a charitable thought, I didn't want another Christian to arrive in the Lord's presence with my trading cards.

After an hour had gone by with not the slightest hint of a rapture, I decided that I'd been had. Jesus wasn't coming. I got up and looked out the window. Outside, kids were running up and down the street playing kick the can in the afternoon light. None of them seemed worried in the slightest about missing Act 2 of the earth's destruction (Act 1 being the flood Noah escaped from). They were laughing and having a good time while I sat inside waiting for someone who clearly had no intention of keeping our date.

Suddenly, the skies clouded over with angry gray. There was a rumble of thunder, followed by a crack of lightning, and it began to pour. The kids scattered as the rain descended in sheets, and darkness fell over the neighborhood. The whole world seemed to be surrounded by the storm. It certainly wasn't what I'd expected the rapture to look like. I'd thought it would be more like *The Sonny and Cher Comedy Hour,* with bright lights and maybe some lively music.

Then a horrible thought entered my mind: What if this wasn't the rapture but the beginning of Armageddon? Every good Baptist child knew that after the beauty of the rapture was the horror of Armageddon, the final battle in which Satan's demons warred with the troops of heaven. It was, we were told, a terrible time, filled with death and fire and long lines at the supermarkets, where only those whose foreheads were branded with 666 — the mark of the beast — would be allowed to buy food. The branding itself might not be so bad, but the trade-off was that, once marked as Satan's plaything, a person would never be allowed into heaven. Being faced with the choice of either starvation or eternal damnation was not something I was keen to have happen.

What if Jesus had already come while I was packing, and now the storm was heralding the imminent arrival of the seven-headed beast with the whore of Babylon astride its back? Oblivious to the departure of the saved, I could have missed the whole thing, and now the apocalypse was upon me. I reeled at the thought that somewhere along the line I'd skipped a step in the process of salvation, and now I was doomed to burn with all the other sinners. Maybe Jesus had sensed my earlier gleeful musings on viewing the punishment of the wicked and decided to leave me behind.

Filled with terror I ran from my room screaming. I half expected the halls of my house to be overrun with lurching demons reaching out to drag me into hell. Holding my arms in front of my face as protection, I dashed into the living room, wailing, "No, Jesus! I didn't mean it! Please, come back! Whatever I did, I'm sorry!"

Sitting on the couch were two women I had never seen before. They looked at me, pieces of cake paused in midair in front of their open mouths. I stopped, gasping in huge breaths, and stared at their anxious faces. They didn't look like demons to me, but I couldn't be sure. I knew the devil and his ways well enough to know his minions appeared in many forms, even as cake-eating middle-aged ladies. "Be gone!" I shouted forcefully, dragging up from my subconscious the words our pastor claimed Jesus used to vanquish the evil ones. I pointed my finger at them defiantly. "In the name of Jesus Christ, go back to hell!"

The ladies looked at me, panting and wild-eyed before them. Then they screamed. Then I screamed. Then I fainted.

The next thing I knew, I was lying in my bed with my mother looking down at me worriedly. "Is this heaven?" I asked hopefully, thinking maybe Jesus, impressed by my stand against the demons, had decided to come back for me after all.

"What?" she said.

"Where are the demons?" I asked.

"What demons?" she said. "What are you talking about? And why did you interrupt my garden-club meeting? You scared Mrs. Whitley and Mrs. Hogan half to death."

Garden club? Then it wasn't really the apocalypse after all. I breathed a sigh of relief. I started to get out of bed.

"Oh no you don't!" my mother said. "You stay right there and take a nap. I think you have a fever."

She left, shutting the door behind her. I looked out the window. It was still raining, but the world wasn't ending. Larry Norman was a big, fat liar. I wasn't sure at first if I was comforted or saddened by this thought. On the one hand, it would have been fun to have seen heaven and found out once and for all what it was really like. Never having met anyone who'd been there, all I had to go on were second-hand descriptions. I wanted to see it for myself. And I had done such a nice job of packing. It was a shame to see it all go to waste.

Then again, there were a few things to look forward to right here on earth. It was summer. I'd just gotten a skateboard and new sneakers I hadn't even worn yet. My father had promised to take me and my friend Stephanie to *Star Wars* for the ninth time. My birthday was coming up, and I'd been hinting around for a bike. Besides, it was the Fourth of July, and I knew there were sparklers in my future when the rain stopped. There was a lot left to do; maybe heaven could wait a while. Satisfied that I wasn't quite ready for Jesus to come back after all, I settled into the pillows and closed my eyes.

Before I drifted off, I looked at the stack of boxes next to the bed. Half asleep, I picked up the box with my favorite *Charlie's Angels* cards in it and tucked it behind my pillow. Just in case.

The Crown of Heaven

The clearest memory I have from my eighth summer is of kneeling behind a station wagon in Mickey Whitlow's driveway and saving the soul of a girl named Susan. I have forgotten Susan's last name — or likely never knew it — but I do remember that she had a pinched face, startling green eyes, and frizzy red hair. We were frequent playmates and usually spent the long July afternoons racing our Big Wheels up and down the street in mad delight.

That summer I was spending several mornings a week attending Vacation Bible School at our church. Vacation Bible School is the Baptist version of summer camp, but without the fun or the mosquitoes. It consisted of sitting on the scratchy-carpeted floor of the basement of Immanuel Baptist Church and listening to our teacher, Nancy Higgins, tell us about Jesus. Nancy Higgins was a college student home on break for the summer. Before assuming the role of teacher, she had been known to the neighborhood kids simply as Fat Nancy, an unkind but completely appropriate appellation. Now, placed in a position of authority, she was determined to get her revenge for our years of torture.

On the first day of Vacation Bible School, Fat Nancy suggested that we each pledge to win over a soul to

Christ by summer's end. Should we fail to accomplish this goal, we would disappoint Jesus in some fundamental way that, she implied, would result in his not liking us very much. She did not quite say that we wouldn't be allowed into heaven, but somehow we were nevertheless left with this impression.

Deciding that I might as well get it over with as quickly as possible, I decided that the most logical choice for my conversion subject was Susan. On the day in question, I took it upon myself to take her down not the road upon which our Big Wheels raced but the much more exciting road to heaven. Fat Nancy had been very explicit in her instructions for soul-saving, and I had memorized the required steps thoroughly.

"You have to pray to Jesus," I told Susan as we knelt on the scratchy asphalt, the tar warm under my bare knees. She looked at me and blinked. "Like this," I said. I folded my hands and tried to appear as earnest as possible. "Dear Jesus," I intoned solemnly, "please forgive me for all of my sins and come into my heart."

Susan repeated my plea in a quiet voice. When she was done, she frowned. "I don't feel any different," she said. "If he's in my heart, shouldn't I feel it or something?"

I nodded. "You won't for a while," I reassured her. "But he's there. Now, no matter what you do, you won't go to hell."

We had spent a long time on hell before getting to the actual moment of salvation. I had described it for Susan in the fullest and grimmest of terms — all fire and burning and endless centuries of torment. I assured her that without Jesus, she was headed there immediately, should she suddenly be struck down by a car while riding her bike or choke to death while downing the contents of a Jumbo Pixi Stik from the 7-Eleven. That, in fact, was what finally sold her on the Son of God and all he had to offer. That, and the fact that I told her that her dog would be waiting for her in heaven when she got there.

"Is that it?" she asked, picking absentmindedly at a scab on her elbow. She seemed to be expecting some big finale, like a musical number or something.

I thought for a minute, staring at our distorted reflections in the slightly rusted chrome of the station wagon's bumper. I didn't want her to go away thinking she'd been cheated. "Now we sing," I offered.

Her face brightened. "What do we sing?"

I chose at random a song I had heard my sisters playing on the stereo. "Don't stop thinking about tomorrow," I warbled. Susan joined in, her thin voice mingling with mine as we chanted the familiar chorus together. "Don't stop, it will soon be here." Thus sanctifying our act with the words of Christine McVie and Lindsey Buckingham, I declared her born again.

That night, during dinner, I told my mother what I'd done. She beamed at me over her meat loaf. "You'll get a jewel in your crown for that," she said as she spooned peas onto my plate.

This was the first I'd heard about jewels, or crowns. All Fat Nancy ever talked about was making Jesus happy. "What kind of jewel?" I asked. I had visions of something vaguely tiaralike, similar to what Miss America wore on her runway walk, or perhaps something more reminiscent of the crown the Burger King wore in the television commercials for his restaurant.

"Was Susan Catholic?" my mother asked.

I looked at her blankly. I really had no idea.

"Was she Jewish, then?" my mother suggested hopefully.

"I don't know," I said finally.

My mother sighed. "You really must find out," she said. "It's important."

"Why?" I asked. Quite honestly, I didn't really know there was a difference. I'd just assumed there were Baptists, like us, and then a general multitude of sinners. Until her salvation by my forceful message of grace, Susan, I had believed, was simply one of the latter. Now, if I was hearing correctly, there were actually categories of the unsaved. Secretly, the thought delighted me no end.

"It's important," my mother explained, "because when you get to heaven, you will get a crown covered with jewels, one for each soul you've saved while you're here as God's messenger. You get different kinds of jewels for different kinds of souls. For Catholics you get sapphires. For Lutherans you get emeralds. For all of those Eastern types like Buddhists and Hindus and whatnot, you get rubies. And for Jews," she said triumphantly, "you get diamonds, which are the best of all. That's because the Jews killed Jesus, and winning one back is very special."

"I think she was Catholic before," I said doubtfully. Although Jews were clearly the bigger prize, to my mind sapphires seemed somehow much more festive than diamonds.

My mother smiled. "That's fine," she said, seemingly satisfied with my achievement. "There are so many of them; it's good when we can show one of them the right way."

I sat through the remainder of dinner contemplating this new information. If my mother was right — and I

had no reason to believe she was not — the choice of
which souls to lead to salvation held far greater importance than merely swelling the ranks of Christ's army.
Where once I had thought it enough simply to snatch
my peers away from Satan's fiery grasp, now I understood
more clearly what was really at stake in the cosmic battle
between good and evil.

As I thoughtfully consumed my meat loaf, I envi-
sioned the crown I would one day wear in glory, the construction of which would be my life's work from that
moment on. Now that I knew the rules, I feverishly
designed in my mind the exact pattern of jewels I would
work toward. Not to be satisfied with any old hodge-
podge of gems, I was determined to meet my Lord
dressed in a smartly encrusted crown of diamonds and
sapphires, with perhaps a hint or two of emerald, if I
could scare up a few Lutherans.

Later that night, alone in my room, I took a piece of
yellow construction paper and cut it into two strips,
which I taped together to form a crown. Using the blue
crayon from my Crayola 48 set, I drew a sapphire onto
the paper. Placing the crown on my head, I gazed at
myself in the mirror over my dresser. Although admittedly only a poor copy of the real crown I was sure was
being forged for me up in heaven, it looked very nice
indeed, if a bit bare. It was time to get started on filling
up the empty space with jewels.

I took out the school annual and found the picture
of my class. I ran my finger down the list of names, counting the numbers of souls waiting for the deliverance I,
with the helping hand of Christ, could offer them. With
a red felt-tip pen, I carefully wrote in *c*'s next to those students I felt must surely be Catholic and *j*'s next to the

ones who seemed, by whatever vague criteria I was using, to be Jewish. Those I was unsure of, such as Annie Chang, received question marks. When I was finished, I had a list of nine Catholics, five Jews, and four question marks. Folding it neatly, I stuck it into my notebook, where I could easily find it when the appropriate time came. Putting my crown on top of my bedside table, I went to sleep.

I dreamt that night of Jesus. He came to me in a long white robe, his face rosy with celestial delight. I approached, and he beamed, his mouth curling into a beatific smile. In his hands he held a crown — my crown — only now it was glittering with blue and white, the accumulated reward of a life spent in faithful service. As I stood before him, holding my breath, he placed it on my head. I felt its weight settle around me and looked up into my Lord's adoring eyes. As the heavenly host broke forth in song around us, he leaned down, bathing me in all his glory.

"Fabulous," he whispered in my ear. "Absolutely fabulous."

The next day my salvation campaign began in earnest. No longer motivated simply by the fear of Fat Nancy's veiled threats, I now had a real reason to spread the word of God throughout my neighborhood. Armed with my notebook and list of names, and fueled by my dream of the night before, I marched straight over to the house of the first kid on my list — Wayne Lerner.

I knew Wayne was Jewish, because the previous Christmas our teacher had given us a brief description of Hanukkah to explain that not everyone sang carols and waited for Santa to come down their chimneys. At the time I had felt sorry for Wayne because he didn't get to have Christmas. Now that I knew Jesus was also absent from his life, I considered it my duty to attend to his salvation as quickly as possible. Besides, I remembered what my mother had said about Jews being worth diamonds. Winning them over to the Lord might be tough, but I was experienced. With my easy conquest of Susan under my belt, I felt no need to warm up by practicing on a few Lutherans first. Ringing the Lerners' bell, I waited patiently until Wayne appeared.

"Hi, Wayne," I said cheerfully.

"Hi," he said. "I'm watching cartoons. What do you want?"

"Want to hear about Jesus?" I asked hopefully, visions of sparkling diamonds floating through my head.

"Jesus?" he said, his face wrinkling into a bewildered look. "There's no such thing as Jesus."

I stared at him, my mouth hanging open. No such thing as Jesus? I couldn't believe what I was hearing. Perhaps, I thought, this wasn't going to be so easy after all.

"But Jesus died for you," I said. "He died for your sins. You have to believe in him or you'll go to hell." Hell had worked wonders on Susan; I hoped it would do the same for Wayne.

"There's no such thing as hell either," Wayne said. This time he seemed very pleased with himself, as though he knew something I didn't.

"There is too a hell!" I yelled, determined to make my point. "And there is too Jesus! You take that back."

Wayne held his ground. "No, there isn't. Jesus is all made up. So is hell. My dad said so."

He had me there. He had his father's word behind him. The only authority I had to back up my claims was Fat Nancy and my mother, and I knew their names carried no weight with Wayne. Frustrated, I resorted to the only weapon I had left in my arsenal. Recalling what my mother had said about Jews, I gave him a menacing look.

"Killer!" I said forcefully, pointing at him. "Murderer! You killed Jesus!"

The next thing I knew, Wayne was flying down the steps. He tackled me, and we fell to the ground, shouting, punching, and kicking. We rolled around in the grass for a minute, both of us yelling our heads off. Then Wayne's mother appeared and managed to pull us apart.

"What's going on here?" she demanded.

Wayne and I scowled at each other. "I was trying to save him from hell," I explained, sure that any intelligent adult would see the reasonableness of this. "I was trying to tell him about Jesus."

"He said I killed Jesus," Wayne said sullenly. "He said I *killed* him."

With Wayne and I in tow, Wayne's mother marched over to our house, where she told my mother what had happened. "He said that Wayne killed Jesus," she said. I hung back, silent, knowing that my mother would side with me.

Instead, she grabbed me by the arm. "Apologize," she said, thrusting me toward Wayne. "Go on — tell Wayne you're sorry."

"No," I said. "I won't. He killed Jesus." Fat Nancy had told us several grim stories about missionaries being persecuted by the very people they were trying to save, and she assured us that suffering for Jesus was just as good as actually saving souls. "Besides, you said...," I began.

My mother pinched me hard. "Say you're sorry," she hissed through clenched teeth. Then she leaned down and whispered in my ear, "If you do you can watch an extra hour of television tonight."

I was confused. My mother was actually encouraging me to lie. It didn't make any sense. Why didn't she want me to stand up for Jesus? Just last night she had told me that the Jews killed Jesus. Now here she was making me apologize for saying so. Wayne and his mother were both staring at me, waiting for me to say something. My mind raced as I tried to decide what to do. I weighed the possibility of an extra hour of television against the reward I might get for standing my ground for Jesus. Then I remembered that *The Love Boat* was on that night. I'd never been allowed to see it before because it was on past my bedtime. I caved in.

"I'm sorry," I said sweetly.

Wayne's mother smiled. Wayne made a face at me. My mother said, "Honestly, I don't know where he comes up with these things." Then the two of them left. Afraid that my mother would revoke her promise if questioned too heavily about it, I left her to her gardening and spent the rest of the day in my room.

That night, after a blissful hour spent watching Gopher and Isaac laugh it up with Charo and Robert Wagner, I went to bed. Again I had a dream where I was wearing a jewel-studded crown. Just as before, I saw Jesus approach me, and I waited to feel his forgiving hand on my shoulder. I knew he would understand why I had done what I'd done. Who could stand firm against the temptation of Charo?

Just before he reached me, Jesus was transformed into the glowering figure of Fat Nancy. She stood over me, her terrible eyes flashing, as she snatched the crown from my head.

"You've disappointed Jesus," she said venomously. "And you lied. He's taking back your crown, and you're going to hell!" The ground beneath my feet opened up, and I felt myself falling into a pit of flames. Above me, Fat Nancy held up my crown and cackled triumphantly as I screamed "I'm sorry!" and plunged to my doom.

Just before I hit the flames, I woke up. I looked around my dark room for the horrible spectre of Fat Nancy as my heart raced wildly. Finding myself alone, I turned on my light. The crown was still on my bedside table. Picking it up, I tentatively placed it on my head. I knew the dream was a warning. I'd been forgiven once, but I couldn't fail a second time. I had to make it up to Jesus.

Opening my notebook, I looked at the next name on my list — So Yung Kwan. Afraid to go back to sleep and encounter Fat Nancy again, I leaned back against the pillows and went over and over in my head exactly what I would say to So Yung the next day when I rang her bell.

The Theory
of Relativity

As queer people we seldom have the advantage, when we are very young, of having role models to guide us in the ways of being successful dykes and queens. Rarely does anyone point out the "spinster" aunt and suggest that the girls of the family emulate her ways, and "bachelor" uncles with their hosts of amusing, witty friends are almost never invited to spend time with their nephews, teaching them the finer points of homosexuality. Still, I've discovered that most of my friends did have at least one family member who, however unknowingly, provided a few hints as to what might be in store for them later in life.

In my family that person is my Aunt Betty. Aunt Betty is my father's sister, the only girl in a family of four boys. Since before I was born, she has lived with her "friend" Doreen in a little house right up the road from my father and his brothers. The house is surrounded by concrete lawn ornaments including, but not limited to, dwarves, frogs, deer, little boys peeing into the air, and even a life-size burro being led by a life-size Mexican man in a sombrero, who long ago was christened "Pedro Pulling His Donkey" by my ribald cousins. Aunt Betty herself is slightly shorter than Pedro and a little taller than his donkey. Her hair has always been cut very,

very short, and she wears cat-eye glasses trimmed in rhinestones.

Doreen looks exactly like Roy Orbison, the singer who sang "Pretty Woman." She wears brown tinted glasses and lots of turquoise jewelry, and she smokes long, brown cigarettes that look like sticks hanging out of her mouth. Because she's smoked so much for so long, her voice is very low and throaty, and she follows almost everything she says with a drawn-out cough. For years she drove a small orange pickup truck, to the hood of which she had affixed one of the small metal bulldogs that adorn the hoods of Mack truck tractor trailers.

When I was younger I liked to visit Aunt Betty and Doreen not because they provided me with any clues to my future but simply because their house is fascinating. See, they collect things. Not the usual stuff, like comic books or baseball cards, or even dead bugs or seashells. Weird stuff. And their collection spans more than five decades. The whole barn behind their house is crammed with plastic model horses, old aftershave bottles shaped like boats and trains, garage calendars from the '50s that have frisky paintings of naked women on them, '60s psychedelic memorabilia, and license plates from every state except Idaho, which Doreen says she finds disturbing because of its fascination with potatoes. The walls are plastered with posters of Farrah Fawcett, Shaun Cassidy, Erik Estrada, and other '70s icons.

The house itself is even more crowded. Over the years the two women have amassed an intriguing assortment of oddities, all of which are prominently displayed. Doreen is the keeper of the museum and delights in showing visitors around. She proudly points out the pictures of dogs playing poker and will wax eloquent about the *Star Trek* memorial plates that line an entire wall. There are boxes of playing cards decorated with film stars of the '40s, Barbies of every shape and size, and even a cabinet filled to overflowing with all manner of Trolls, those big-bellied, genderless, plastic figurines sporting shockingly bright tufts of hair.

But the thing Doreen loves most is her collection of Elvis spoons. She has a whole rack of them that hangs in the living room next to the plate commemorating the wedding of Prince Charles and Princess Diana. Every time anyone comes to visit, she has to drag the person in to see the Elvis spoons. "Look," she says, holding them like they were the frozen embryos of extinct animals, "this is The King when he was thin."

If she's really on a roll, Doreen will take down every one of her twenty-two spoons and explain where she was when she got it, what The King is doing on it, and how much it's worth (not that she'd ever sell). Sometimes she puts on Elvis records and sings along, twisting around the room belting out "Heartbreak Hotel" in her raspy voice while the long brown cigarette smokes away and her turquoise earrings glitter in the lights.

The saddest moment in both Aunt Betty's and Doreen's lives was when The King died. They had tickets to the concert he was to perform the next night. Now framed, these tickets hang in a place of prominence over the fireplace, and every so often during a visit one or the other of the women will touch them gently and begin to cry. "It's so tragic," she'll say before moving on.

When I was a child, my favorite thing to do when visiting Aunt Betty and Doreen was to sit at the giant player piano on the screened-in porch and work the pedals that made it turn. Aunt Betty had found somewhere an enormous stash of music for the piano, and I would spend hours fitting the punched-paper cylinders into the playing mechanism and listening to the songs. My favorite was "Talk to the Animals," from *Doctor Doolittle*, and I practically wore it out playing it repeatedly, pumping the pedals faster or slower to see what effect it had on the melody, until inevitably one of the adults would come out and ask if didn't I maybe want to stop now and do something else. Years later, when I first saw a bunch of queens sitting around a piano singing show tunes, I would have flashbacks to those days on the patio and wonder if it was entirely coincidental that songs like "Oklahoma" and "Over the Rainbow" had been left out on the bench before I came by.

Along with the curiosities, Aunt Betty and Doreen also collected small dogs. In particular, they were very fond of Pomeranians. When I was little they had two Poms. One was large and white and called Honeybun; the other was small and orange and called Dee-Gee. I adored Dee-Gee and Honeybun, but they hated me unequivocally. Clever little beasts, they'd developed a system to their torture so that no one suspected their malice toward me. When I would arrive they would be all happy barks and wagging tails, and it was always suggested that I sit in the living room with them while the adults had coffee. But the minute I was left alone with the pair, they chased me up onto the plastic-covered sofa, where I would stand, looking down at them, as they bared their sharp little teeth and growled as only small, incredibly fuzzy dogs can do.

Things picked up slightly when Doreen brought home another dog, a pug that was christened Jada. Jada was as friendly as Dee-Gee and Honeybun were terrifying. She snorted and licked her way around the house, bullying the Poms and getting into everything. I loved her pushed-in face and curled tail and took to her immediately. I was not, however, allowed to pick her up. According to Aunt Betty, if I did, her little bug-eyes would immediately pop out of her head. The vet, she said, had shown her how to pop them back in, but she didn't want to take any chances. Horrified at the thought of an eyeless Pug and two little eyeballs rolling about on the kitchen linoleum, I restricted my affections for Jada to petting.

But the greatest curiosity in Aunt Betty and Doreen's house at that time wasn't the dogs, or even the player piano, but Doreen's aged mother. Mrs. C, as she was called, came to live with her daughter after she drove her car into a pond and it was decided she was no longer able to take care of herself. Thus she was packed off to the palace of lawn ornaments and small dogs, where she was installed in the guest bedroom.

If I was afraid of Dee-Gee, Honeybun, and Jada's unpredictable eyes, I was positively terrified of Mrs. C. She had been born and raised in England and had about her a decidedly regal air. Combined with the fact that she had long ago become irretrievably insane, she was formidable indeed, especially to a very small boy. She insisted, for instance, on being served afternoon tea, complete with sandwiches and a steaming pot of Earl Grey, every single day. The rest of her time was spent sitting in her room, watching game shows and waiting for visitors who never came.

My one vivid memory of Mrs. C occurred on a day when I had decided once and for all to see what would happen if I did indeed pick up Jada. I had begun to suspect that the popping-eye story was not entirely true, and when I was left alone with the dog while Doreen and Aunt Betty went into the garden for a minute, I saw my chance to put it to the test. Gripping Jada firmly around the middle, I began to lift her off the floor. I did it slowly, with the idea that if her eyes did begin to slip out of her head, I could probably put her down again before they tumbled out completely. I had lifted her front feet off the floor with no ill effects when suddenly I heard a shrill voice behind me.

"You there, boy. What are you doing?"

I dropped Jada and whirled around. Standing in the doorway to the kitchen was Mrs. C, clutching a handbag. Her hair had been put up in a rapidly falling pile, and her cheeks were rouged the color of cotton candy. Other than that, she was stark naked. All I could do was look at her wrinkled body in sheer terror.

"The queen," she announced loudly, stepping into the kitchen and pointing a long, thin finger at me. "The queen will be here in fifteen minutes."

With that, she squatted on the floor and released a small stream of urine, which pooled under her. She then stood up, turned, and went back to her room. When Aunt Betty and Doreen returned a few minutes later, I was still standing there, mouth open, staring at the puddle on the floor.

"What's that?" Doreen said suspiciously, eyeing Jada, who was hiding under the table.

I couldn't speak. I didn't know how to tell her that her mother had just made wee on the floor.

"Um, I don't know," I said. "It just sort of…happened." It sounded completely unconvincing, even to me.

Doreen grabbed a wad of paper towels and began to wipe up the mess. She never mentioned the incident again, but I had the distinct impression that whenever I went over there she kept one eye on me at all times.

It never occurred to me, when I was young, that Doreen and Aunt Betty were lesbians, mainly because I didn't think much about the subject at all. But even if I didn't know about Aunt Betty, she certainly knew about me. One afternoon, when I was about twelve, I was alone with her in the kitchen. She was washing dishes, and I was playing with Jada. For no apparent reason she turned to me and said, "I just want you to know that life is very hard for people like us." I nodded, unsure of exactly what she meant, and she went back to washing dishes. Like the puddle of pee, we never spoke of it again.

It took me many years to realize that while I found them delightful and fun, other people in the family thought Aunt Betty and Doreen were just plain strange. They came to all the family events and were even included in the annual Christmas Secret Santa swap, where everyone drew names out of my Uncle Dick's John Deere cap and bought gifts for whomever they picked. But slowly I began to notice that when they were spoken of, it was with a tone of faint puzzlement, as though no one could quite figure them out. Their relationship to each other was never discussed, even though my father and uncles had themselves built the bedroom addition onto the house and installed in it the single big bed the two women shared. Nor did anyone ever really answer when I asked, as I did several times, why Aunt Betty had never married.

My mother in particular had a strong dislike for the couple, especially for Doreen, whom she found positive-ly frightening. She refused to go to their house and avoided them at family functions after saying a quick hello. The year she drew Aunt Betty's name for her Secret Santa, she made my father switch names with her. Once, when during a heated argument my sister said, "You know, I'm starting to think Aunt Betty is the only normal one in this whole family," my mother began to sob uncontrollably and ran from the room. At the time, I couldn't understand why.

Many years later, when I was old enough to know about both Aunt Betty and about myself, I would discover that my mother's stepbrother was also gay. When my mother's mother died, David and his lover, George, attended the funeral. At the house after the service, my mother stood tensely in the living room while David and George took over the kitchen and organized the cleaning up. I knew she was upset at having two of "them" (my grandmother had adored the men, by the way) in her mother's kitchen, but she couldn't do anything about it. I desperately wanted to go in and talk to them, but I was too frightened.

As we stood there, my mother wishing David and George would leave and me wishing they'd take me with them, my mother looked across the room at my grandfather's sister, who was talking forcefully about politics as her daughter sat meekly by her side. "I don't know why she has to be so loud," my mother said irritably. "I don't know what her problem is."

Just then, Aunt Betty came up to us. Overhearing my mother's comment, she snorted. "Her?" she said. "I'll tell you what her problem is — she's a goddamned dyke. She tried to pick me up at the service."

For my mother this was a moment of pure horror. For me it was a wonderful revelation. We were everywhere. As my mother quickly left to get away from the growing number of queers in her midst, Aunt Betty turned to me and laughed. "She had that coming," she said simply and took a bite of her Jell-O salad. I went home that night pleased beyond words. For the first time I understood just why those old garage calendars and Elvis spoons had made me feel right at home all those years. I thought about my own fascination with things like old cigarette advertisements featuring film stars and statues of the saints, and it all started to make sense.

Unfortunately, David and George were both killed in a car accident a few years later, before I ever had a chance to ask them everything I wanted to. As for Aunt Betty, she still lives in the little house with the lawn ornaments. The dogs are long gone, as is Mrs. C, but the Elvis spoons remain, and Doreen continues to polish them regularly. Whenever I go home, I can be sure that when I drive by, the two of them will be sitting on the porch smoking their long, brown cigarettes.

Sometimes I think about what my life would have been like if I hadn't had Aunt Betty's peculiar presence in my life to, knowingly or not, reassure me that being different from everyone else around me was okay after all. And sometimes I think about her and her strange house and strange lover of almost forty years, and I wonder about the possibility that it runs in the family. My nephew is showing a decidedly queer bent these days, and he spends a lot of time at that old player piano. Is it a sign? I sure hope so. After all, someone has to inherit the Elvis spoons.

Saying Good-bye to Grandma

My grandmother took a long time to die. Bred from hearty Irish stock, she survived a succession of strokes, heart failures, and other maladies that would have felled a rhino, despite the fact that she was barely four feet tall, weighed no more than sixty pounds, and subsisted almost entirely on a diet of Mountain Dew and Girl Scout cookies. Although doctor after doctor assured her children that she couldn't possibly make it through another year, she refused to pass on, outliving even the miniature dachshund my aunt bought to comfort Grandmother in her last days.

When she finally started to go, she required almost constant care, a task no one in my father's family was eager to take on, having already endured her for nearly eighty years. Finally, it was my mother who volunteered for death watch, and she devoted much of her time to attending to the old woman in the last months of her life. None of us really knew why she did it. Maybe it was because, under the numbing influences of the painkillers they gave her to quiet the angry voice of the cancer inside her, my grandmother finally became the mother-in-law my mother had wanted in the first place: one who wasn't able to harangue her with a steady stream of complaints and accusations. More likely it was simply that my mother enjoyed the opportunity to have her enemy just where she wanted her for a couple of hours a day — flat on her back and incapable of getting away. I have happy, if unfounded, visions of her leaning over the recumbent figure of the old woman and whispering in her ear, "Let's see you criticize the way I baste a turkey now, you miserable witch," before dancing gaily about the room.

Whatever her reasons, when the end came my mother spent many hours with the woman who bore my father, I suspect asking her what she had done to make him the way he was. She administered medications, gave sponge baths, and sometimes just read to grandmother from the endless stream of religious tracts left by the local clergyman who, tipsy from his lunchtime "tea break," would frequently spend a hazy hour or so with my grandmother talking about how wonderful it would be for her to finally see her Lord. Somewhere along the line, my Irish-Catholic grandmother (she had been sent to a convent at a young age but somehow managed to be impregnated by my English grandfather while still behind its walls) had switched her allegiance to the Baptist church, which was also my mother's denomination of choice. I think my mother always felt slightly offended by this, as though Grandma were trying to horn in on yet another area of her life, and secretly hoped there would be a mix-up in the heavenly paperwork that would prevent her quarrelsome in-law from ever achieving eternal rest.

Still, my mother went every day. Usually she would go over sometime in the early afternoon to the house where my grandmother was playing out her last dramatic scenes, returning around suppertime with updates on the death watch. Generally there was nothing much to report. But one night when she came home, my mother had an unusually chipper air about her. She whistled as she came in the door and greeted us with unusual warmth.

"Oh, lord," my father said instantly. "She died, didn't she?"

My mother laughed lightly. "No, not yet." She removed a piece of paper from her pocket and waved it at us. "However, we did discuss the imminent event in detail this afternoon."

"That looks like a napkin," my father said, squinting.

My mother unfolded the paper, which we saw was decorated with festive red and green poinsettias. "It is a napkin," she said. "It's all I had to write on when she started talking."

"Talking about what?" I asked.

My mother smoothed out the wrinkled napkin and smiled. "Her funeral plans," she said. "She decided this afternoon to arrange her funeral, and she asked me to write it out for her so that everyone would know what she wanted."

"You're kidding," my father said, shocked but obviously impressed by his mother's unfailing ability to organize everything around her even as she stood with one foot in the grave and the other on rapidly eroding ground.

"No, I'm not," my mother answered. "It's all here in black and white. Well, red and white anyway. All I had in my purse was a marker."

"What does she want?" my father asked.

My mother fair near radiated joy as she looked at us and delivered her pronouncement. "She wants to be buried in the pet cemetery."

"The what?" my father asked, incredulous.

"The pet cemetery," my mother repeated. "You know, the one behind Dick's house."

My Uncle Dick had, in fact, created quite an extensive burial ground in the wide grassy field behind his tool shed. Presided over by a lovely cement replica of St. Francis of Assisi, who according to Catholic legend (despite their mother's conversion, the children, with the exception of my father, were all staunchly Catholic) had done something miraculous involving swarms of animals, the graveyard was a repository for all of the deceased family pets. As each one died, Uncle Dick fashioned for it a cunning tombstone, which he spent days carving by hand and inscribing with the dead pet's name, dates of birth and death, and sometimes a clever saying. My family was quite fond of pets, and over the years there had been quite a number of dogs, cats, birds, assorted rodents, and even the odd snake and frog that had gone to their rewards. Each one rested now in the pet cemetery, immortalized by epitaphs such as MUFFIN 1960–1966: CATS HAVE NINE LIVES; HE GAVE UP AFTER SIX or AMY 1970–1984: A FAST DOG, BUT THE CAR WAS FASTER.

"She wants to be buried in the pet cemetery?" I said, both shocked and secretly thrilled.

My mother nodded firmly. "She says the dogs were the only ones who ever loved her, and she wants to be surrounded by them forever." I could tell she was trying not to laugh.

"She's nuts," my father said simply. "She's just nuts."

"That's not all," my mother continued. "She says that she wants to be cremated—"

"What's so odd about that?" my father interrupted.

"—and she wants the ashes placed in her garden gnome," my mother finished.

My father looked at her blankly. My mother, no longer able to contain herself, was shaking with laughter as tears streamed down her face. The garden gnome had long been a sore spot in family history. It had originally been given to my grandmother by my Aunt Betty one Christmas. Approximately three feet tall, it looked like any other concrete garden gnome commonly found in the gardens of people — like my relatives — for whom that sort of thing is of ceaseless interest.

Except that his particular gnome had been painted to resemble turquoise-colored marble. It's wizened little features had been glazed an unearthly blue-green and then streaked with black to create the ultimate specimen of white-trash high art. The gnome was holding in its stunted arms a small flowerpot, in which it was expected that one would plant geraniums or pansies or some other cheerful flower. It was into this pot that my grandmother wished her earthly remains to be placed.

The garden gnome had caused trouble from the moment it came on the scene, topped with a bright red bow and waiting under the tree during the annual holiday gift exchange. My father, thinking it a joke, had made some unkind comment about it looking a bit like a midget with an advanced case of blue balls. My aunt, who had spent many hours at Mimi's Ceramics Studio achieving the marbled finish, burst into tears. It had been a tense moment and one that was not spoken of again, for fear of bringing up even more bad feelings. My grandmother, for her part, had placed the gnome in a position of honor in her yard, where it had remained until she became ill, at which point my father wrapped it in burlap and hid it in the darkest recesses of the barn. Now, with her final death wish, my grandmother threatened to reopen old wounds.

Still, the idea of my grandmother being forever embraced by the arms of her beloved gnome and resting among a bevy of dead pets was funny. I started to laugh along with my mother, who was by now too far gone to stop. Even my father cracked a smile. "Of course she can't do that," he said, vainly trying to appear genuinely astounded.

My mother gave a great heaving sigh and wiped her eyes. "And why not? It's her last wish — I think we should respect it."

Ultimately, the issue of the gnome was put to a family vote, and in the end my mother stood alone against the assembled aunts and uncles, all of whom found the idea absolutely appalling. When my grandmother died a few weeks later, she was indeed cremated, but the ashes were then buried with great ceremony alongside her husband, whom she had never really liked, in the family plot. There was no statue of St. Francis, no merry little headstone with a witty epitaph, no garden gnome. But the relatives were happy. It was probably the one and only time they had ever dared defy her.

Later that day, during the immense feast that inevitably accompanied any family event, whether it be a birth, wedding, or death, my mother took me aside and showed me a small jelly jar filled with dust. "It's some of her ashes," she said, shaking it for effect. "I took them from the box this morning when no one was looking. Come on."

While the rest of the family sat inside enjoying their pasta salad and reminiscing about Grandma, we crept out to the barn. Heaving the gnome into a wheelbarrow, we wheeled it out to the old pet cemetery and placed it among the deceased pets, between an ancient setter and a guinea pig. My mother took the jar and put it in the gnome's flowerpot.

I looked at the gnome's hideous grinning face. "He looks demented," I said.

My mother laughed. "Give him a week with her," she said. "He'll be certifiable."